BOOK THREE: GEHENNA

BLACK SWAN

MARK GOODWIN

ACKNOWLEDGMENTS

I would like to thank my Editor in Chief Catherine Goodwin, as well as the rest of my fantastic editing team, Jeff Markland, Frank Shackleford,
Stacey Glemboski, Sherrill Hesler, and Claudine Allison.

CHAPTER 1

For wickedness burneth as the fire: it shall devour the briers and thorns, and shall kindle in the thickets of the forest, and they shall mount up like the lifting up of smoke.

Isaiah 9:18

More than two months had passed since Shane's violent skirmish with Harvey Hammer. Shane and Bobby arrived at the sheriff's office Thursday morning. The building, which normally buzzed with activity, was silent. Like the rest of Sylva, NC, the office was perilously close to becoming a deserted ghost town.

Johnny Teague, the new sheriff, stood up from his desk. "What are you boys doin' here?" A glass coffee pot was on the counter behind him. The burnt smell mingled with the staleness of an all-but-abandoned building.

"Reporting for duty." Shane adjusted his pistol belt.

Johnny pressed his lips and studied Shane as if concerned. "You boys just came back from a fuel run last night. Don't you think you ought to get some rest?"

"Somebody has to do it," Shane replied.

"Sabas and Thompson are both on." Teague walked out from behind the desk.

"Two cops for the entire county?" Shane inquired.

"What did Caleb Creech have to say?" asked the sheriff.

"The UN is setting up shop across the river from him in Huntington," Bobby replied.

Johnny shook his head. "I'm sure a giant fuel refinery would be a hard thing for them to miss."

Shane nodded. "Creech says it's a matter of time until they show up on his doorstep."

"What's he planning to do?" asked the sheriff.

Shane walked over to the coffee pot but decided against having a cup of the singed, sooty brew. "He said he'll hold them off as long as he can. Even with all the foreign contractors, the UN is spread pretty thin. I'm sure Maris Allard would rather not have another failed city, especially one that has the reputation for being as docile as Huntington, West Virginia. The Economic Stability Commission has already lost control of Atlanta, Miami, Chicago, Philly, LA, even Charlotte. If the ESC starts losing their grip on towns like Huntington, Allard will have no credibility whatsoever."

Bobby leaned against the desk. "Creech has what it takes to turn Huntington into an open insurrection against the UN and the ESC. It would be in the best interest for all involved to find a compromise."

"Well," said Johnny Teague, "Creech is a union negotiator. If anyone can do it, he can."

Shane added, "Yeah, he said he'll look for someone near the top of the food chain to bribe. If that doesn't work, he'll resort to intimidation."

"And if that doesn't work?" Johnny asked.

"Scorched earth." Shane shook his head. "Said he'll burn the whole thing down. Said it will look like Gehenna."

"What's that?" inquired the sheriff.

Shane replied, "It's a valley outside of Jerusalem, where the people used to burn their trash in the time of Christ. Before that, Jews used it to sacrifice their children to Baal and Molech. The place is considered cursed by God because of all the innocent blood spilled there. In Jesus' time, rabbis used Gehenna synonymously with the word *hell,* because it was always burning. In the original Greek, Jesus uses it in Mark 9, but it's translated as *hell* in the King James and other versions.

"According to Creech, it will take months for the oil and gas to burn out if he decides to set the refinery on fire, thus his allegory."

"Where did you learn all of that?" Johnny asked. "Gehenna, I mean."

"Pastor Joel taught on it once." Shane paused to look out the window. "But Creech seems well-versed in that particular bit of history also." Two motorcycles drove past. Shane caught a glimpse of black leather jackets and faded denim.

Johnny walked up to the window. "That's the second time I've seen those two drive by. Jimmy said he saw them cruising up Main Street yesterday."

"Rough lookin' pair." Bobby craned his neck to watch the bikers pass by.

"That's why we need a show of force," said Shane. "They're looking for a target. Did you get a good look at the patches on the back of their jackets?"

Johnny stepped back from the window. "Jimmy said they're from Charlotte. Iron Devils, I believe."

"Do you know anything about that gang?" Bobby inquired.

"Drugs, guns, and motorcycles." Johnny returned to his seat. "If you two insist on volunteering six days a week, why don't you see if you can bring them in?"

"On what charges?" Shane asked.

"I'd have to imagine they're doing something wrong," replied Johnny.

"What would be our reasoning in pulling them over in the first place?" Bobby inquired.

Johnny lifted his shoulders. "You'll think of something. Affiliation with a known criminal organization will do if they don't give you anything else to work with."

"Then what?" Shane asked. "The jail is already overcrowded. We can barely feed the people we've got locked up now. Butterbean works 12-hour days, six days a week."

"I know." Johnny sighed to show his exasperation. "At the county commissioners' meeting last night, Brady Watkins suggested horse whipping the non-violent offenders and setting them free."

Shane fought a smile, shook his head, and rolled his eyes. "Brady Watkins, the old mountain man with half his teeth missing?"

"Teeth or no teeth, he's a commissioner." Johnny grinned. "And his suggestion seems to be catching on around town."

Shane laughed and looked out the window. "Horse whipping!"

"It worked for the Romans. People can't pay fines with no money. Most are in for property crimes. We don't have any way to handle probation. Phone service is out. We have blackouts about half the day." Johnny looked up at the lights overhead as they flickered, then went out. "See what I mean?"

"I didn't say I don't like the idea. But it's going to go over like a burp at a prayer meeting." Shane considered what a public whipping might look like.

"I say go for it," Bobby chuckled.

Johnny seemed to be attempting to maintain a serious tone. "Jimmy said he'll support the proposal. He's going to recommend making it optional."

"Optional?" Shane dropped his brows.

"Yep, anyone who wants out of jail can take ten lashes. Conditions are pretty rough in there. I think anyone who qualifies to get out will take the whipping."

"Ten lashes and they're home free. I'd take it," Bobby said.

"Me, too," Shane added. "But do you think it's enough to keep them from coming back?"

"Second offense is twenty-five. If they get a third offense we'll run the perpetrators out of town. We'll shoot on sight if they're caught in Jackson County after that."

Shane shook his head. "I can't imagine how many state and federal laws we'll be violating with the whipping, forget about the shoot-on-sight order."

"We're all trying to make the best of a bad situation," said the sheriff. "If the commissioners pass the ordinance, Greg would be considered non-violent. He'd be eligible to go free."

Shane's jaw clenched. "Non-violent? He nearly got my entire family killed!"

"I know, indirectly," Johnny held up his hands.

"I don't want that piece of filth out on the streets!" Shane said.

"Okay," said Johnny. "What if we escalated him directly to excommunication?"

"Meaning what?" Shane asked grimly.

"Meaning since his actions contributed to the deaths of several people, he gets 25 lashes and has to vacate the county immediately upon his release."

Shane considered the option. "If he comes back, it's shoot on sight."

"If he comes back," said the sheriff.

"I'll mull it over. I hate thinking that my sister is still legally married to this scumbag." Shane pinned the metal badge on his plaid shirt.

Shane watched Bobby pin on his badge. "If you've got a car for us, we'll get to work."

"Car is right out front. It's gassed up, thanks to you boys." Johnny handed him a set of keys. "Call if you have trouble. We might be short-staffed, but we can have half the men in the county in a posse if you run into anything."

"Thanks." Shane led the way to the parking lot.

Once in the vehicle, Shane started the engine and pulled out of the lot.

"It's going to be a hot one today. Better get a little fresh air while we can." Bobby rolled down the passenger's side window.

Shane opened his window as well, figuring it would allow him to hear the sound of the motorcycles if they were nearby. "You don't have to work six days a week if you don't want to. It's not like you're getting paid for it."

"I know." Bobby let his heavy arm rest in the window as he rode. "But if you can do it, so can I."

"I appreciate that, but you don't have to. I feel guilty for dragging you along."

"Don't. I know why you work so much."

"Oh yeah? Why is that?" Shane looked across the seat at his companion.

"You don't like to be around the farm. I don't blame you. It would be a painful reminder for me if I were in your shoes."

The statement struck a nerve, but Shane said nothing.

Bobby was quiet for some time, then added, "But you'll eventually have to find your peace."

"Why is that?"

"Because of Cole. He's lost a lot, too. He needs his dad. You've already missed out on so much of his life, you don't want to lose much more. It's okay to grieve those you've lost, but you can't let it get in the way of the life you have with those who remain."

Shane tightened his jaw. "I've never known you to be so philosophical, but thanks for reminding me of all the time I missed being a father to Cole."

"My intentions weren't to rub salt in your wound. I just want you to consider what you're passing up in the here and now."

"I know." Shane sighed. "Thanks."

"Did you hear that?" Bobby asked.

"Yep." Shane punched the accelerator. "Motorcycles. Sounded like they're in the direction of Main Street." He picked up the radio. "Deputy Thompson, this is Shane Black. We might need back up near Main Street if you're in the area."

"We can be there in about ten minutes," Thompson replied. "What's going on?"

Shane quickly relayed the sheriff's desire to bring in the bikers for questioning, then formulated a plan with Thompson.

Shane turned onto Mill Street. Bobby picked up the radio and called Deputy Thompson. "Roland, we've got the bikers. They're headed west on Mill."

"We're coming off the expressway right now at Dillsboro."

Shane said, "Have them wait on one of the side streets in Dillsboro. We'll close the gap, hit the lights and see what happens."

Bobby relayed the message.

"10-4. Set the trap, and we'll be waiting," Thompson replied.

Shane sped up to get closer to the pair of bikers. He turned on the red and blue lights of the patrol car, but the motorcycles accelerated rather than pulling over.

"Surprise, surprise," Bobby said.

The bikes turned left and Shane followed. Bobby picked up the radio. "They're heading right toward you. They just turned on Depot Street."

"Good. You've got them cornered either way. If they've scouted out the area, they'll know Hemlock is a dead-end," replied Thompson.

Shane smiled when the bikers turned onto Front Street. "Have Thompson cut them off as soon as we pass Church."

Bobby pushed the talk key. "Okay, we've got them. Close off the intersection of Front and Webster."

Shane watched the other patrol car pull out from behind cover, blocking the path of the two bikers. Shane turned the car sideways to eliminate any possibility of escape for the bikes. Both of the gang members stopped their motorcycles.

Shane called over the intercom, "Drivers, shut off your engines and step away from the bikes."

The two men looked at the patrol cars on either side of them before complying with the demand. Shane and Bobby exited their vehicle with pistols drawn, as did Deputies Thompson and Sabas.

"Get on the ground!" Shane yelled.

One of the bikers protested, "Whoa, man! Chill out! This is a traffic stop, not a drug raid!" He was tall and thin with a long grey ponytail, a thick gray beard, and wore a heavily-soiled, red bandana on his head.

Shane shook his head. "A traffic stop is when the police turn on the lights and you pull over. You lost the accompanying customary courtesies when you forced us to set up a roadblock."

The other rider was more robust. He wore a similar beard, with shorter hair, and likewise had a filthy red bandana functioning as a sweatband. "We didn't see you behind us. It ain't like we led you on a high-speed chase."

"Speed limit is 20 through town. We were doing 60 and still couldn't keep up," said Shane. "Not only was it a high-speed chase, but 40-over is also considered reckless driving."

"Come on man, this town is all but abandoned. We've seen like two stores open around here," said the tall one. "Say, ain't you that guitar player?"

"Yeah! That's him!" The other biker pointed at Shane.

The tall one asked, "Is this one of those prank TV shows?"

Shane nodded. "Yeah, we're filming a celebrity version of Punk'd in the middle of the apocalypse. The country has no functioning currency, phone service is out, nationwide rolling blackouts, and society is melting down into abject chaos, but people still gotta laugh, right?"

The tall one began chuckling. Shane holstered his weapon and approached the two men. He jerked the thin biker by the shoulder of his leather jacket. "Get on the ground!"

Shane forced the biker to the pavement while Bobby wrestled the other to the asphalt. Shane turned his head away as he placed the handcuffs on the biker's wrists. The rancid smell of sweat seething from the man's clothing and body was not merely a product of this single hot July day. Rather, the acrid fumes represented weeks of poor hygiene, fermented perspiration left to sour day after day in the warm humid climate of the North Carolina mountains. "First thing we're going to do is hose you boys down. Smells like you might have missed your bath last month."

"This one's got a pistol." Bobby held up a small-caliber semiautomatic.

Shane patted down his detainee. "This one has a revolver." He pulled the pistol out of the man's waistband. ".38." He continued checking the prisoner's pockets. "What's this?" Shane held up three small baggies of a white crystalline substance.

Deputy Ricky Sabas looked on while standing guard. "Looks like meth."

Shane jerked the lanky man up and shoved him toward the patrol car. "Come on. Let's go."

"I hope you know what you're doing, Deputy," said the scroungy biker. "We ain't up here alone. You might be invitin' more trouble than this little Podunk town can handle. By the time this is all over, you'll be writing a country music song about how not to tangle with the Iron Devils. If you live through it, that is."

"Is that a threat?" Shane asked.

"Fair warning is all."

Shane shoved the man's head into the roof of the

patrol car. "Watch your head." He propelled the man into the back seat and slammed the door.

CHAPTER 2

Say to them that are of a fearful heart, Be strong, fear not: behold, your God will come with vengeance, even God with a recompence; he will come and save you.

Isaiah 35:4

Shane stopped by the little cabin after his shift. He knocked gently on the door. Julianna soon answered. "Hey, how was work?"

Shane provided a short narration of arresting the bikers and processing them into the jail.

"You shaved their beards and their hair?" Julianna stood with her mouth open.

"We weren't going to shampoo them, and we certainly weren't going to put them in that

13

overcrowded jail in their present condition. We'd risk contaminating the whole facility."

"And that was your call? To make them look like military recruits?"

Shane smiled. "Those fellows needed a little discipline in their lives."

"But it was an affront to their identity as bikers. Unless you're planning to give them a life sentence for three grams of meth and two pistols, you'll eventually have to let them go. When they get back to their group, revenge will be at the top of their list of priorities." She paused for a moment. "You're a good leader, but you're impetuous."

"I know," Shane replied. He thought about the brash decision to raid Hammer's compound which had cost the lives of Bivens, Pastor Joel, and so many others. He recalled the hasty move to Nashville for which he'd sacrificed his relationship with Julianna. "I don't always think things through."

"It's good to be decisive. Few things are more dangerous than analysis paralysis, particularly in this environment. But, it doesn't hurt to mull things over a bit, weigh out the pros and cons," Julianna added.

"You're right. I will. However, we might not have to wait for them to get out for that revenge thing you were talking about."

"How so?"

"Snake, that's the tall thin one's name, he said they weren't up here alone. He mentioned that the whole gang was in the area."

"That's just great." She nodded.

"Yeah, so, in my defense, I'm not sure it was even possible to make matters worse. At least we know what they're up to now."

"And what's that?" She held up a finger. "But real quick before you answer, for the record, you didn't help matters either."

"Point taken," he agreed. "Coot, that's the stocky one, he said they were looking for a new center of operations. Evidently, MS-13 and the Bloods are fighting for control of Charlotte since UN peacekeepers declared it a failed city. Seems like the Iron Devils can't even survive in Charlotte without the thin blue line to keep things civilized. Thus, they've decided to scout out our fine little enclave."

"So, what's his name again?"

"Coot."

"Right, Coot. So, Coot *volunteered* all of this information."

Shane bobbed his head from side to side. "You could say that."

"Under duress?"

"Under a high-pressure water hose shooting ice-cold water." He added, "Naked."

"That'll do it." She crossed her arms. "And what's the sheriff planning to do about that?"

"He's passing the word around. Telling all the men in the county to be on high alert. Everyone who volunteers at the sheriff's department takes a radio home. We'll all be monitoring it round the clock. If an incident arises, we all have a list of people to notify on our way to the call."

"Shane!" Cole came to the door. "Are we going

to pick vegetables in the garden?"

"Sure." Shane ran his hand across Cole's hair. "Get your bucket."

"Aunt Angela said she'd make a clobberer if we can find enough blackberries."

"You mean a cobbler?"

"Mmmhmm." The young boy nodded.

Shane smiled. "Okay, we better get another bucket then."

Cole disappeared to fetch his containers.

"Mosquitoes are bad," said Julianna. "Don't have him out there too long."

"If he'll eat more onions, they'll bother him less."

"I'm doing good when he eats green beans. Onions are a stretch."

"We'll go up by Mom's herb garden. I'll rub some thyme on his neck and arms. That will help. Peppermint, too."

"Are you sure you should be going up there?"

"He'll be okay. I'm not sure he really understands what happened. But either way, it's something he'll have to learn to deal with."

"I was talking about you." She spoke with a tender tone.

Shane smiled. "I'll be fine. I have to learn to deal with it also."

Cole soon returned with his buckets. "I'm ready."

Julianna kissed her son on the head. "Be a good boy."

"I will!" He waved and tagged alongside Shane to the garden.

***

Friday morning, Shane and Bobby headed into work. "Did you think any more about what I said?" asked Bobby.

"About what?" Shane tried to recollect the prior day's conversations.

Bobby rolled down the truck window and let his arm rest on the door. "About working less, spending more time around the farm with Cole."

"Once we get this biker thing sorted out, I'll give it some more thought. But, I am going to make sure I'm spending at least an hour a day with him. We picked blackberries and gathered vegetables from the garden yesterday evening."

"Feels good, right?"

Shane turned the steering wheel. "Yeah, it feels good. Thanks for encouraging me on that."

When they arrived at the sheriff's office, Shane noticed three customized Harley Softail motorcycles parked out front. "Looks like Coot and Snake have visitors."

"What's the plan?" Bobby asked.

"Lock them up. Let them have a visit." Shane parked behind the bikes making it difficult if the riders tried to leave.

Shane and Bobby walked inside to see Butterbean dealing with three people, all wearing leather vests with Iron Devils patches on the back. The one in the middle had slicked-back blond hair, muscular arms sleeved in tattoos and wore jeans much cleaner than those of Coot and Snake. On his left was a shapely woman in skin-tight jeans with black boots. She also had blond hair and tattoos down to her wrist. To his right was a towering wall of a man. Shane guessed him to be nearly 7 feet tall and pushing 400 pounds. Even Bobby seemed small in comparison.

Butterbean was in the middle of a high-pitched, nervous attempt to convince the bikers that their friends were not being held at this particular institution. "I done told y'all, we ain't got nobody named Coot nor Snake!"

"It's true," Shane whispered to Bobby. "That's not their given names. So he's technically not lying."

Bobby shook his head. "Yeah, but Butterbean still can't sell it."

"Can I help you folks?" Shane spoke with a loud voice.

The muscular one in the middle turned around. He had a manicured blonde beard and tattoos on his neck. "We're looking for some boys who were out this way yesterday."

"And Deputy Ritter told you they weren't here?"

The girl and the giant both turned around as well. The man in the middle said, "That's what he's claiming."

"You don't mind if we frisk you folks do you?" Shane took a deep breath, hoping his own nervousness wouldn't show.

The giant nudged the one in the middle with his elbow. "Scotty, you know who that is, don't ya?"

"No," he replied.

"Shane Black." The girl looked Shane up and

down and ran her tongue along the edge of her teeth.

"Right in front of me?" Scotty glared at the girl.

She snarled. "It ain't ever stopped you."

"Okay, so who is Shane Black?" Scotty stared at Shane.

The big one answered, "He's the guitar player for Backwoods."

"Oh! Okay!" He snapped his fingers. "Mud Flaps! Right? I love that song!"

Shane tried to capitalize on his celebrity to defuse the situation. "Yeah. This here is Bobby. You've already met Deputy Ritter. I guess you're Scotty."

"Yep. Scotty Scofield. This is Ox, and Tessa is my girl."

"Good to meet you." Shane gazed past them to Butterbean who was behind the bikers playing charades. He seemed to be mimicking the process of racking a shotgun. Shane assumed it was a question so he gave the most subtle nod possible. "I'm afraid I'm still going to need to frisk you folks."

"Since we're all friends now, why don't we just treat each other with mutual respect?" Scotty smiled.

"I'd love to, but it's department policy." Shane let his hand rest on his pistol.

"You always insult visitors like this?" asked Tessa.

"Normally, no. We have metal detectors at the front door, but with the power being out and all, we have to perform a manual pat-down." Shane watched as Butterbean slowly and quietly pulled the shotgun out from behind the desk.

"It's a violation of our rights. We refuse." Scotty put his hand in his pocket. Ox and Tessa followed suit in lowering their hands.

Shane unbuttoned his holster. "I'm afraid I'm going to have to insist."

"You sure about that, Mr. Black?" Scotty seemed ready to draw.

"It's Deputy Black to you." Shane gripped the handle of his Glock. "Butterbean!"

Butterbean racked the shotgun and the three bikers froze in their tracks.

"Put your hands on your heads," said Shane.

"You going to arrest us?" Scotty asked.

"Just going to frisk you." Shane kept his voice calm and even.

"Everyone is packing heat. In case you haven't noticed, it's a dangerous world out there," said Tessa. "But as long as I'm getting frisked, can I request that Deputy Black be the one to do it?"

Scotty seemed to get more agitated. "I'm not going out like this."

Shane's pulse quickened. "Deputy Ritter will search Tessa."

"Me?" Butterbean's voice betrayed his anxiety.

Scotty turned to him, pulled his empty hand out of his pocket and pointed to Butterbean. "If you put your fat fingers on my girl, you chubby little perv, I'll…"

Shane seized the opportunity to draw his weapon, as did Bobby. Shane yelled, "Hands on your head, right now!"

Ox pulled a pistol out of his pocket. BOOM! Butterbean fired the shotgun, spraying Ox in the chest. Shane watched the giant to see what he would do next.

Ox dropped the pistol. "You shot me!" He seemed surprised.

"Hands on your head!" Shane yelled at Scotty and Tessa. "Bobby, get the cuffs on Ox. Butterbean, rack that shotgun! The next one that steps out of line, blast 'em."

Butterbean's face was pale white with red blotches. He racked another shell into the chamber and nodded profusely with eyes as wide as patrol car hubcaps.

Shane cuffed Scotty, then Tessa.

"Ohhhh!" Ox cried in pain. "I'm bleedin' bad!"

"Y'all have to get him to the doctor!" Tessa exclaimed.

"Healthcare ain't what it used to be around here." Shane removed a pistol from Scotty.

"You still want me to search Ms. Tessa?" Butterbean's voice quaked as much as his hands.

"I'll take care of it," said Shane. "You keep that shotgun ready."

"I'll wring your fat neck for shooting Ox! You better hope he doesn't die!" Scotty growled at Butterbean.

Shane slapped him in the back of the head. "In case you haven't figured it out by now, Ox isn't the first person Deputy Ritter has shot. He probably won't be the last either. See how he's shaking? If you keep rattling his cage, he might accidentally blow *your* head off."

Shane retrieved another small semiautomatic from the back of Tessa's waist. "Bobby, Butterbean, watch them. I'm going to call the hospital on the radio."

Shane walked to the desk and picked up the mic. "This is the sheriff's department. I've got a gunshot victim. Is anyone available at the hospital?"

Seconds later, Johnny Teague's voice came over the radio. "Shane! What happened? Who's shot?"

"Some bikers came in looking for their friends. One of them drew a gun on us. Butterbean shot him."

"Y'all are alright?" asked the sheriff.

"Yeah, but we probably need to bring in some more deputies. We might have more visitors soon."

"Oh, you can bank on that!" Scotty interjected. "If you don't let me go, my boys will burn this town to the ground!"

"You have to get Ox to the hospital!" Tessa exclaimed.

Shane called again. "This is Deputy Black, I need someone from Harris Regional. Anybody, please pick up!"

"Hello?" came a young female voice.

"Hello, who is this?" Shane asked.

"Maggie. I'm a volunteer."

"Good. I need you to send an ambulance to the sheriff's department."

"We don't have any drivers. You have to bring the patient here."

Shane looked at the mess. "I can't. We have other prisoners who need to be processed. I can't leave them unattended. Who is the doctor on right now?"

"Dr. Akers. It's him, two nurses, and myself. We're completely overwhelmed right now."

"Tell Dr. Akers that we have a gunshot victim. Take the radio to him."

"Hang on." The girl's voice went silent.

"You have to get him to the hospital!" Tessa continued her protest.

Ox had fallen unconscious and the puddle of blood was becoming a pond. Shane waited for the doctor.

"Shane." Finally, Doctor Akers answered. "What's the situation?"

Shane explained the wound.

"Sorry," the doctor replied. "If all of us committed the next four hours to working on him, we probably couldn't save him from a shotgun blast to the chest. Plus, we've got other critical patients who would be jeopardized if we even tried. We simply can't help. If you can send someone over here, I could give them a hypodermic with something for pain in case he comes back around. Otherwise, I can't do anything for the man."

"Thanks, Doc." Shane put the radio on the desk. "Let's get these two in a holding cell."

Scotty rolled over. "No way! You're not locking me up while Ox bleeds out on the filthy floor!"

"Then Deputy Ritter is going to shoot you!" Shane pointed at him. "From what you've told me, I've got a biker gang heading this way. I'm not wasting time on you."

Scotty ceased his objections and allowed Bobby to help him up and escort him to a cell. Shane followed behind with Tessa while Butterbean guarded the dying giant.

CHAPTER 3

Stand fast and prepare yourselves, for the sword devours all around you.

Jeremiah 46:14b NKJV

Shane shook Jimmy Teague's hand when he arrived. "Thanks for coming in, Mr. Mayor. I'm sure you're aware that it would be best for the town if you weren't here."

"Yeah, Johnny tried to tell me that." Jimmy looked at the growing number of citizens and deputies filling the sheriff's department. "But I think the best thing for the town is to have all hands on deck. Do we know how many of them to expect?"

"Around 200," Shane replied.

"And you're sure they'll come here?"

"Scotty Scofield is the gang's founder. They know he's here. Busting him out is their primary mission."

Jimmy nodded. "Then I guess this is our Alamo."

Julianna and Dan were the next people to arrive.

Shane's brows knitted together. "Who's watching the farm?"

"Nobody." Julianna walked passed him. "Everyone else went to the Teague compound. Angela is watching Cole."

Dan patted Shane on the back. "Mrs. Betty offered so we took her up on it. I can't imagine they'd have trouble out there, but if they do, Mrs. Betty can watch the kids while the girls hold the fort."

"I suppose that's best." Shane looked up to see Johnny Teague coming through the door. "How many people were you able to round up, Sheriff?"

"Another twenty or so. Said they'd be here as soon as they can." He looked around the office. "What was our last count?"

Shane looked at Julianna and Dan. "These two make forty."

Johnny frowned. "That's a far cry from even numbers."

"True, but we do have a couple of things going for us," said Shane.

Johnny looked at Bobby who'd just returned from the jail. "Is he always this optimistic?"

"Not always," he said.

"Let's hear it," the sheriff said to Shane.

"For starters, Grindstaff is the only way into the complex."

"Unless they attack on foot," countered the sheriff.

"From what I've seen of this bunch, they don't do much on foot. The founder is all jacked, but I'm guessing that's 20 percent from working out and 80 percent from steroids."

"What else?" asked Johnny.

"Motorcycles provide very little in the way of cover. The riders will be easy targets."

Johnny tilted his head. "I'm not sure I'm expecting them to circle the building like a tribe of Indians on horseback. I think they'll find cover when they arrive."

"When they arrive, yes," said Shane. "But they have to get here first."

"I'm listening," said the sheriff.

"We should put a roadblock at the entrance off Grindstaff. We can have the entire road up to the sheriff's department lined with snipers. We can pick off half of them before they ever get to the building."

"So, you propose we open fire as soon as they turn into the drive?"

"Absolutely. We should make it abundantly clear that trespassers will be shot on sight, then live up to that promise."

Johnny looked at Julianna, Bobby, and Dan. "The sniper team will eventually be overwhelmed by the sheer number of bikers."

"That's when I'll call retreat," Shane explained.

"Calling retreat and having it as an available option are two different things. It'll be like trying to snatch a marble out of a hornets' nest."

"We'll need a secondary team of snipers on the roof to provide cover fire long enough for us to get back inside," said Shane.

Bobby added, "We can have patrol vehicles lined up in such a way as to give us temporary cover for our retreat."

The sheriff looked at the floor and smoothed the edges of his mustache. "I don't like it, but I can't think of anything better. Take whoever you need and set up your ambush outside. I'll start putting together a team for the roof."

"Any volunteers?" Shane asked.

Julianna rolled her eyes. "You know I'm coming."

Bobby lifted his shoulders. "I've always got your back."

"I came to fight," said Dan. "Count me in."

***

Four hours later, Shane swatted at a mosquito buzzing around his ear. "I wish someone had brought something to drive off these bugs. Nothing will be left of us by the time the Iron Devils show up."

"When do you think that will be?" Dan looked through his rifle scope.

"Your guess is as good as mine. But we'll hear them when they're coming. They'll have to come off the expressway. That should give us at least a five-minute warning."

"I bet they wait until dusk." Julianna sat with her back against a tree and her rifle propped up between her legs. "Since their vehicles leave them so exposed, the cover of darkness is their best bet."

Bobby sat on the opposite side of the same tree with his rifle across his lap. "Then again, they might decide to abandon their comrades. Someone is always lookin' to move up in these types of organizations. Having Scotty out of the way might be somebody else's wish come true."

Shane slapped another mosquito. "A magic fairy might bring me a can of mosquito repellent and a gallon of ice cream, too, but I'm not counting on it."

Minutes later, Jimmy walked up. "I brought you some of Mama's herbal bug balm."

"No kidding!" Shane stood up to see what the mayor had to offer.

"Yep." He pulled the lid off of an old yogurt container. "Get you a dab and wipe it on your neck and arms. It'll keep them little buggers away from you."

Shane stuck his fingers into the oily concoction and began applying it liberally to his wrists and collar. The pungent odor smelled of mint and spice. "What all does she have in this?"

"Peppermint, lavender, clove. Some other stuff, but I don't know all of it."

The paste felt greasy. "What is she using for the base?"

"Lard," said the mayor.

Shane paused for a moment after realizing he'd been smearing pig fat all over himself, but soon recalled the annoyance of the mosquitoes and helped himself to another glob of the piquant goop.

"You didn't happen to bring any ice cream, did

you?" Bobby grinned.

"No." The jest fell flat on the mayor who looked at Bobby as if he might be suffering from heatstroke. "Y'all make sure you stay hydrated out here. I'll send someone around with food in an hour or so."

Shane passed the container of bug balm around to his companions. "Okay. Thanks."

***

Shane awoke to the buzzing noise from a distant armada of motorcycles. The sun had set and only the faint glow of dusk remained in the evening sky. "I must have dozed off after dinner." He stood up and checked his rifle.

Julianna stood facing the direction of the expressway. "You were entitled to a nap."

"You'll be glad you grabbed one while you could if this thing lasts into the night." Bobby pulled open the hook-and-loop closure on the front of his tactical vest to expose the butt of a fresh magazine ready for a quick exchange.

Dan pointed to the road spikes at the entrance of the sheriff's department parking lot. "That will be the first place they stop."

Shane nodded. "We'll wait until they get off their bikes to move the spikes. That demonstrates intent to trespass. Once they've done that, we can open fire."

"Do we keep shooting even if they turn and flee?" Bobby asked.

"Yep. Once they put their hand on those road

spikes, they've crossed the Rubicon." Shane flipped the safety off of his rifle. "Just because they pull back doesn't mean they won't be coming around for a second strike. We have to take every opportunity we get to even up the numbers."

Shane listened to the roaring engines get louder and louder. "Here they come! Everybody down!"

Julianna, Bobby, and Dan all lay down flat on the grass and took cover behind trees. Shane waited a few more seconds to catch a glimpse of the invaders before finding his preselected fighting position. He knelt behind a towering pine which had a bushy rhododendron next to it for added concealment. Shane eased his body to the ground as the bikers got closer. With a loud whisper, he addressed his team. "Remember, don't shoot until they move the road spikes."

Shane watched as the first line of motorcycles raced up Grindstaff Cove Road. Six bikers riding adjacent to one another took up both sides of the road. Behind them, the lines weren't as tight, but they filled the pavement with no less than four bikes across at any given point in the procession. Shane shook his head and whispered to himself, "Looks like a swarm of hornets."

The lead bikes did not slow down when they turned into the entrance of the sheriff's department. The first seemed oblivious to the road spike until it was too late. They all slammed their brakes and lost control of their bikes which skidded into the metal chain-link road spikes. The next line of riders was also unsuccessful at bringing their motorcycles to a halt. They careened into the first line of men and machines, adding to the melee.

Finally, the third wave stopped their bikes as did the successive waves.

A stocky rider from the front row got up from the crash and screamed a tirade of profanities as he looked at his mangled motorcycle with its headlight still shining. He had a bald head and a long handlebar mustache. Next, he stepped in front of another bike's headlamp to examine the bad case of road rash on his right arm and shoulder. The skin had been unevenly peeled away by the pavement and stripes of blood were just beginning to appear. "Get these wrecked bikes out of the way and somebody move these spikes!" He paid no attention to two other riders who had fared much worse in the collision than himself. They seemed unable to walk on their own and other bikers helped them to the side of the road.

Shane made eye contact with the rest of his team. He gave a hasty nod then turned his attention back to the uncoordinated mob trying to clear the roadway. Shane led the assault by firing first. He picked out a target among the gang members still seated on their bikes, knowing they'd be in the best position to retreat once the shooting began. POP! POP! POP! He hit three before anyone knew what was happening. Next, he searched for the heavy bald man with a long mustache. Shane set his sights on the man and unleashed a volley of shots. However, he failed to hit the moving target who disappeared into the roadside brush.

Julianna, Bobby, and Dan also succeeded in clearing out a number of the Iron Devils. Shane didn't stop to count the dead but figured there to be at least thirty bodies lying on the asphalt. Several of the gang members rode away on their bikes, while still others abandoned their motorcycles and took cover in the shrubbery across the drive from Shane's team.

Shane switched magazines. "Keep pressing them! Don't give them a chance to get organized!" He released another fusillade of lead and fire toward the fleeing Iron Devils.

Julianna paused her assault and crawled to Shane's position. "That was a good ambush. We killed or incapacitated no less than forty of them. I think we should fall back to the building."

Shane wanted to keep up the attack but knew the four of them could be overwhelmed in a matter of seconds. "Okay, Julianna and Dan, you two bound back to the first patrol car. Bobby and I will cover you while you move. Yell *set* when you get there, then cover us while we move back to the second vehicle; just like we practiced."

Dan and Julianna crouched low and sprinted for cover. Shane and Bobby sent a wave of projectiles downrange to keep the enemies' heads low.

"Set!" yelled Dan.

"They're coming!" Julianna opened fire at the hostiles emerging from the shrubbery. "Hurry!"

Shane heard bullets whizzing by in both directions while he charged toward the cover of the vehicle.

"We aren't going to make it to the second car!" Bobby shouted beside him.

Shane pointed toward the patrol car where

Julianna and Dan were positioned. "We'll hold up here until we can fend them off."

Shane slid behind the cover of the vehicle and took out his radio. "Johnny, we could use some help from the boys up top about now."

The sheriff's voice came back. "You're still too far away and down the hill. We can't see you to provide cover fire."

"We're a quarter of the way up the drive toward the parking lot, behind the first patrol car. The Iron Devils are closing in from the northeast. Just start peppering that area."

"*You're* northeast!" said the sheriff. "We're liable to pepper your team. You're just going to have to make it up the hill. Once you get to the third patrol car, we can cover you."

"Everybody heard that?" Shane asked his team.

"It's not getting any easier. If we gotta go, we better do it now!" Bobby pulled the trigger of his AR and let off ten rounds in short succession.

"Everyone, change mags. Julianna and Dan go first!" Shane slapped the butt of his magazine, seating it firmly in the mag well. "Go!"

Bobby and Shane shot while Julianna and Dan ran.

"Set!" Julianna yelled.

Shane and Bobby sprinted as fast as they could to the next vehicle. Once there, Shane gasped for air. He examined himself and his teammates. "Everyone okay?"

"Yeah, we're good," said Julianna.

"We'll have to cut down speed for the next maneuver," Shane paused from shooting to yell out directions. "One person will fall back while the other three provide cover. Otherwise, same concept. Dan goes first, Julianna second, then Bobby. I'll bring up the rear."

He made eye contact with all of them to make sure they understood. Each nodded. "Good," said Shane. "Get ready!" He replaced his magazine. "Go!"

Dan darted out from cover while the other three bombarded the approaching enemy. "Set!" he yelled from behind the third pre-positioned cover vehicle.

"Julianna, run like you've never run before!" Shane begged.

She gave him a faint smile before jetting out from behind the patrol car.

Again, the other three fired their weapons while Julianna made her bid for safety.

"Don't dillydally." Bobby patted Shane on the back when it was his time to go.

"You don't have to worry about that." Shane fired under the car for the best possible protection.

"Set!" Bobby yelled.

Shane's time to move had come. But while the rest of the team was falling back, the Iron Devils were gaining ground. Shane could see five men taking cover behind the first patrol car, getting ready to pursue him as soon as he came out from behind his temporary fortress.

"Shane, you gotta go now!" Julianna reiterated the direness of his circumstance.

Shane took a deep breath. "I have to trust my team." He looked up. "God, help me, please!" Shane shot out from behind the car like a rabbit.

Shells cracked behind him and projectiles whizzed past his ears.

He felt a round hit his foot. His already-stressed adrenal gland kicked into overdrive. Shane rolled behind the vehicle and dropped his rifle. He grabbed his leg and looked down.

"What is it?" Julianna paused from shooting. "Are you hit?" Her eyes showed deep concern.

Shane examined his foot. He pulled back on the dangling heel of his boot which was shredded by the projectile. He let out a sigh of relief. "It only hit the heel. The bullet didn't go through." He looked up once more. "Thank you, Jesus!"

"It isn't over yet." Julianna shouldered her rifle. "Keep shooting."

Shane nodded and picked up the radio. "Johnny, we're all behind the third car. You should be able to help us out."

"10-4." Three seconds passed between Johnny's transmission and a wave of lead and fire cutting into the enemy from overhead.

Shane used the assistance to change magazines once more. He turned to join in the fight. "What the heck is that?" He watched a large recreational vehicle thunder up the long drive from Grindstaff Cove Road.

"It's an RV with metal plates." Bobby's face took on an expression of utter bemusement.

Shane shook his head. "How does that thing even have the power to move under all that weight?"

"Bikers are notorious for being gear heads." Dan wore a look of amazement at the homemade tank. "They probably switched out the transmission and the engine. I'm guessing they gutted all the furniture also. I bet they ain't got nothing but the steering wheel and the captain's chair left inside."

"And a small army," Julianna added.

Shane watched the vehicle roll all the way up near the front door of the building. It seemed unscathed by the small arms fire coming from the rooftop. "We're cut off!"

Shane called over the radio, "Johnny, are you seeing this?"

"I'm seeing it, but I still don't believe it."

"Where are those two .50 cals we pulled from the raid on Hammer's compound?"

The sheriff replied, "One is back at Pop's place. The other one is here. Locked up down in the evidence room."

"Why isn't it up on the rooftop where it would actually do us some good?" Shane snapped.

The sheriff could be heard barking orders to set up the giant machine gun. Finally, he answered Shane, "I didn't think of it. I was under the impression that we were having a shootout with people on motorcycles. Besides, we don't have much ammo for it."

Shane launched his retort. "It would have cost us nothing to have set it up, just in case."

Johnny replied, "You're right. I should have thought of it."

"Your neglect may very well cost us our lives. Good job, sheriff!" Shane was furious.

"Let's focus on getting through this. If you want my job when we're done, you can have it. If memory serves me correctly, it was offered to you and you turned it down. But that's a discussion for another time."

Shane felt remorseful for berating the sheriff. "I'm sorry. I didn't think of it either. You're right. Let's just get through this."

CHAPTER 4

O God the Lord, the strength of my salvation, thou hast covered my head in the day of battle.

Psalm 140:7

Shane looked past the sights of his AR-15. He took shots at three Iron Devils who'd come from the inside of the up-armored RV. "We can't get around this monstrosity, and it's blocking our path to the building."

"We need to melt into the trees and try to get away," Dan fired at two other gang members sprinting for cover behind the second patrol car.

Shane let off another round of gunfire toward the invaders coming out of the homemade armored personnel carrier. "No way. They'll hunt us down like dogs. Besides being outnumbered, they've got bikes and can cut off all of our possible escape routes."

"Then we have to hold them off until Johnny gets the heavy machine gun set up." Julianna launched another volley of rifle fire toward the encroaching threat.

Shane watched the steel-encased camper rolling in their direction. "I hope that happens soon. It looks like they're coming right for us."

The heavy vehicle edged ever closer, providing cover for what Shane guessed to be twenty gang members walking behind the mobile fortress. "We have to target the feet of the hostiles on the other side!"

Julianna, Bobby, and Dan all joined Shane in lying on the ground and shooting at the feet and ankles of their attackers.

"They figured out our tactic. They're getting back inside the RV!" Dan exclaimed.

"Good! Maybe that will buy us enough time for the sheriff to set up the .50 cal!" Shane said, "I know better than to get too hopeful, but it's something."

Bobby added, "This is my last magazine. The sheriff better work fast."

"I'm out, too," Julianna said.

Shane patted the empty pockets of his tactical vest and nodded grimly. "We're going to have to run right past it. We need to do it now. If we wait any longer, they'll be on top of us."

Bobby looked at Shane with a solemn expression. "No matter what happens, I wouldn't change a thing."

He forced a smile. "Me, too, big guy." Shane turned his attention to Julianna, hoping against certain death that at least she'd make it safely to the building. He pressed the talk key. "Sheriff, we're coming in. Have the door open for us."

"Give me five more seconds," Johnny replied.

"I can't. We've gotta move now." Shane pointed to Dan. "You lead. Julianna in the middle. Bobby and I will cover the rear. Ready. Set. Go!"

The flashes of illumination coming from the tripod-mounted machine gun on the roof of the sheriff's department gave Shane the impression that he was running under a strobe light. The deafening explosions preceded a hail of tremendous lead daggers which cut through the thick steel plates of the improvised armored vehicle. Shane scrambled toward the entrance of the sheriff's department, firing wildly at the enemy all around him while he ran.

Deputy Thompson held the door for Shane's team. "Come on! Come on!"

Shane dared not to hope for his own survival but felt a spark of joy when he saw Julianna cross the threshold into the building. But the enormous gun on the roof kept spitting out wave after wave of destruction which served to quell the aspirations of the enemy. Shane watched Bobby make it to the building. He closed the gap and the safety of the refuge grew closer. Then, he stepped through the door. Johnny grabbed him by the tactical vest and jerked him away from the opening. Next, Thompson and Sabas stood a large metal desk up on end to provide a barrier against the attack.

Shane fought to regulate his breathing while checking to see that Julianna wasn't hit. Once he felt confident that she was indeed safe, he looked over Bobby and Dan. He then offered his hand to Johnny. "Thank you."

"Glad you made it." Johnny smiled.

Jimmy's voice came over the radio. "They're bringing in a second armored vehicle. The guys on the roof are down to three boxes of ammo for the big gun."

Johnny pressed his talk key. "Okay. Have them keep the .50 cal loaded, but let's hold off using it until we know we need it."

"How are we set for a prolonged siege?" Shane asked.

Johnny frowned. "We've barely got food for the prisoners. None of us were counting on being stuck in here."

"Yeah, I certainly never imagined they'd pull anything like this." Shane scrutinized the missing piece of heel from his boot, then turned his attention back to the sheriff. "I recommend putting prisoners on one meal per day. We need our strength. We should get two meals a day so we can keep up the fight. Until we come up with a plan to get out, we're trapped in here."

"I second that recommendation." Julianna held her hand up. "Except for the Iron Devils we have in custody. They shouldn't get anything until this is resolved."

"Agreed." The sheriff nodded. "I'll get someone to do an inventory of what we have so we can make an educated guess about how long we can hold out."

He looked at Deputy Thompson. "The jails should be on lockdown anyway, so have Butterbean take care of getting those numbers together for me."

"10-4." Deputy Thompson left to deliver the orders to Butterbean.

Julianna ran her hand across Shane's back. "I'm going to get cleaned up while the power is still on."

"Sure." He watched her walk away then took a seat in the waiting area.

"Your team has been through the wringer," said Johnny. "We'll get some cots set up for y'all so you can get some rest. We'll hold down the fort tonight and try to figure something out in the morning."

"Thanks. I hope they don't hit us tonight. I don't have much fight left in me. But if they do, make sure someone wakes us up."

Johnny chuckled. "If they hit us tonight, I doubt you'll need a wake-up call."

***

Shane awoke to the sound of Julianna's voice.

"Shane?"

"Yes?" He rolled over to see her lying on the cot next to his.

"Are you asleep?" She turned onto her side with her hand under her head.

"Not anymore. What time is it?"

"4:00 AM. But we've been asleep since 10:00."

"Did you need something?"

"I shouldn't have woken you."

"It's okay. What did you want?"

She rolled onto her back and stared up at the

ceiling. "After the fire at the big cabin, Cole asked me if we were ever going to be safe again."

He sighed. "What did you tell him?"

"I said yes, like a good mother. But I don't know. What do you think? Are we ever going to be safe again?" She turned to face him once more. "Is this all there is, to survive one attack after another?"

"No. We'll get through this. Things may never go back to the way they were, but times will get better."

"Thanks." She pulled the blanket over her shoulder and turned to the other direction. "For making me feel better, that is."

She didn't prod him for an explanation. Rather she seemed to accept his statement as gospel, much in the same way that Cole had accepted Julianna's answer, Shane supposed. He lay on his back for another thirty minutes but couldn't go back to sleep. He eased out of the cot and put his boots on, careful not to make a sound. He moved with precision to pick up his rifle and tactical vest, then rolled his feet, heel to toe, until he'd exited the sleeping area.

Once out into the main office area, Shane found the mayor milling about, quietly going from guard to guard, as if getting updates about what they might have observed from each of their posts. Shane walked up to him. He kept his voice low because of the people sleeping. "What's happening?"

"The gang is set up all around us. Once in a while, one of our guys will spot a glowing cigarette or a flashlight beam. I'm guessing they've got tents or tarps set up out in the woods."

Shane walked to a window and looked out. "Any idea how many?"

"If your information was correct about the original size, should be about 150 left."

"To our 60."

"55," the mayor corrected. "A few of the boys who told Johnny that they were coming never showed up."

"How are we set for supplies?"

"We can hold out for about two days, but I hope we can find a solution before then."

"Temperatures have been flirting with 90. Power is out for at least half the day. Let's pray we can keep the AC going, otherwise, it's going to be downright stifling in here."

"Yep, we'll crank the AC up and cool the building as much as possible while the power is on."

"Any ideas on how we're going to get out of this?"

"Once the sun comes up, we'll start trying to snipe off any of 'em that stick their head out."

Shane pressed his lips together. "So, basically, whack-a-mole."

"I know. It's not the best plan. What do you propose we do?"

"They'll figure out our strategy pretty soon after daybreak. Even the most ignorant will make sure they're not visible to snipers. We won't get more than a handful like that." Shane shook his head. "I can't think of anything better right now. Something will present itself sooner or later. We'll just have to be ready when the time comes."

Shane walked down to the jail's kitchen.

"Shane!" Butterbean woke up suddenly from napping in a chair. "Is everything okay?"

"Yeah, everything is fine for now. But I'm starving. What do you have to eat down here?"

"The trustees will be fixin' up some grits in a while." Butterbean stood up. "We don't have much else. "Some dehydrated potatoes, cans of fruit cocktail, biscuit mix. We cleaned the cooler out months ago. With the power off and on all the time, it wouldn't keep nothin' no how."

Shane looked at the sparsely stocked shelves. "Mind if I get into one of those cans of fruit cocktail?"

"Help yourself." The heavy-set fellow passed him a can opener.

"It would be good if we could figure out a way to get the inmates to start gardening. It wouldn't be much different than working on a road crew."

"It's a good idea," said Butterbean. "But we ain't got nobody to watch 'em."

"Yeah. But if we're going to keep a correctional system running, we'll eventually have to figure something out."

"The sheriff said he hopes people will donate food once the crops start coming in."

"That's not reliable, and it's not fair. If we could fence in that big field between here and Dills Cove, we could walk them right over. I'd think most of the prisoners would see it as a privilege to get outside. We'd have to put in the hard work of erecting the fence, but it would be a one-time investment. If they produced excess food, we could give it to the deputies for payment."

"I like that idea!" Butterbean perked up.

Shane dished out some fruit cocktail for the robust deputy. "We have to get through this siege first."

***

Three hours later, Shane and Julianna lay on their stomachs on the roof of the sheriff's department. Julianna held her rifle while Shane watched through binoculars for opportunities to take a shot at a gang member.

"It's gonna be a hot one," Julianna commented.

"Yep. I can feel the humidity already. I feel bad for the people who get the afternoon shift on the roof." Shane directed the field glasses down to the up-armored camper. "The Iron Devils have scribbled a radio frequency on a piece of cardboard. They put it on top of the RV."

"Let's go call them!" Julianna inched her way back toward the roof access opening.

"We've gotta get Jimmy and Johnny. I'm guessing the Iron Devils are going to list their demands." Once inside the building, Shane led the way to the first level.

Shane found the mayor and the sheriff, then relayed the frequency.

Johnny keyed it into the radio then addressed the gang. "This is the sheriff of Jackson County. We got your message to call."

"Good," said a gravelly voice.

"Who am I speaking with?"

"Bonus," came the reply.

Shane looked at the sheriff and the others, bewildered by the odd name. "The voice sounds the same as the big bald guy with the handlebar mustache. We heard him cussin' out the other guys when he wrecked his bike on the way in."

"We need to be the one issuing the demands," said Jimmy.

Johnny nodded in agreement, then pressed the talk key. "Mr. Bonus, we need you and your gang to leave Jackson County by sunset this evening."

"It's just Bonus. But why would we do such a thing as that?"

"Because if you don't, we're going to start killing your fellow gang members," replied Johnny.

"We don't negotiate with cops or townies," said the rough voice.

Johnny looked at the others but did not press the talk key. "Townies?"

Julianna shrugged. "He lost me at Bonus."

The radio chirped once more. "We demand that you release the prisoners. In return, we will allow you to live."

"That's fairly vague," Johnny replied. "Are you saying you want your members back and that you'll leave the county if we grant your request?"

"No," said Bonus. "I'm telling you to release all the prisoners you have in custody. And we won't be going anywhere. We've decided to make Jackson County our new home."

"I can tell you, that isn't going to happen," said Johnny.

Bonus' reply came quickly. "Then I suppose

we'll have to start rounding up fair young maidens from the county until we get a hold of one that means something to one of you in there. I'm sure I don't have to inform you that not all of the Iron Devils are of the highest character. It will be difficult for me to ensure the safety and preservation of virtue for any young ladies who might come into our custody."

Shane felt a surge of rage bubble up inside. "We have to nip this thing in the bud. We need to empty the machine gun and rip up those two armored campers. Next, we have to charge out there and hunt down the survivors."

"We'll lose." Jimmy shook his head. "We'll lose badly."

Shane remembered the costs of his impetuousness and took a deep breath. "We have to think of something. We can't just sit here while they pillage and rape the town, literally!"

"I agree," said Johnny. "We need to let them know that we're not going to be intimidated."

Shane snapped his fingers. "What did we do with the big biker? The one Butterbean shot in the chest?"

"He's zipped up in a body bag downstairs. We never had a chance to dispose of the body," said Johnny.

"Then let's chop his head off and lob it over the roof. Tell them they have one hour to clear out."

Jimmy grimaced and looked at Julianna, as if expecting her to shiver at the suggestion. She did not, however.

On the contrary, Julianna was the first to offer

support for the idea. "It lets them know that we've thrown out the official handbook, and that we're now operating under the rules of survival."

Johnny crossed his arms and shuttered. "Who's going to cut the head off?"

The four of them looked at one another for a few seconds. Finally, Shane said, "It was my idea. I'll do it."

Johnny gave a nod of appreciation. "I think we've got some Vicks VapoRub around here. That will help cover the smell."

Shane followed him to the desk to retrieve the ointment, then walked down to the kitchen to get a garbage bag and a large chef's knife.

Bobby caught up with him on the way to the basement. "Hey man, you need some help?"

"You don't want any part of what I have to do," said Shane. "But thanks for offering."

Bobby trailed close behind him. "I already know about the mission. If you can deal with it, then so can I. Besides, I played football in high school."

Shane paused on the way down the stairs. "What does that have to do with anything?"

"You're going to need to get the head over the RV. I'm just saying, I've got a pretty good throwing arm."

"I hadn't thought of that. Maybe I'll take you up on the offer." Shane steeled himself for the task at hand. "But I'll take care of liberating the head from the body. This is my burden to bear."

"I won't fight you for that privilege, but I'm here if you need me."

Once at the bottom of the stairs, Shane opened

the door and looked at the large shiny black bag filled to capacity on the cold concrete floor. "I guess I better get to it."

***

An hour later on the roof, Shane handed the garbage bag to Bobby. "How are you going to do it?"

"I was going to take it out and toss it over there, but it would be much easier to use the bag to sling it."

Shane looked on sympathetically. "Easier and less disgusting. But I'm afraid they won't recognize the significance if it's still in the bag. It won't look any different than a watermelon unless they feel so inspired to go look inside. But if it's out, they won't be able to mistake it for anything else. I doubt anyone else in the world has a head that big. They'll know that it's Ox."

Bobby lowered his gaze. "Okay. Do you have a pair of nitrile gloves or anything?"

Shane felt horrible for asking such a despicable favor of his faithful companion. "Yeah. I had a feeling that they might come in handy."

Bobby put the gloves on which fit him more snugly than they would've most people.

"Remember, I threw up twice while cutting it off. Even if you barf once, you've still got me beat."

Bobby untied the plastic bag. "Twice? You're not counting the six episodes of dry heaves?"

"No," said Shane jokingly. "The very definition of the dry heaves is the inability to vomit. Of course

51

they don't count!"

Bobby seemed distracted by the light-hearted jesting. He seized the opportunity to reach in the bag. He extracted the giant bloody head by holding the hair and instantly slug it over the side of the building.

The entire process seemed like one fluid motion to Shane who was impressed by the decisiveness in the task's execution. He watched the wretched thing land with a thump on the roof of the RV, then roll, and come down on the far side of the vehicle. "Wow! Talk about maximum effect! Were you aiming at the roof?"

Bobby stood bent over with his hands on his knees, as if fighting the urge to get sick. "No. Just kinda worked out that way."

CHAPTER 5

Every kingdom divided against itself is brought to desolation; and every city or house divided against itself shall not stand.

Matthew 12:25b

Shane sat on the opposite side of the desk in the sheriff's office, flanked by Bobby, Julianna, and Jimmy. Johnny looked at all of them before pressing the talk key on the radio. "Bonus, I hope you know by now that we're not bluffing. We'll be sending another head out in an hour or so."

Bonus replied, "You're only making things harder on yourself."

"My question is whether or not you're authorized to make the kind of decision which will cost the founder his life."

Bonus said, "We're all prepared to die. Scotty Scofield is no better than anyone else."

"I find that revelation rather enlightening," said Johnny.

"How so?" asked Bonus.

"He seems to command a certain level of—fidelity. At least from what I've seen out of the other inmates associated with your organization."

"Our loyalty is to the club," said Bonus. "Not to any one individual."

"So, you're willing to sacrifice Tessa, Scotty, Coot, and Snake for the honor of the club? Doesn't sound very loyal to me. I think we could reach an agreement that perhaps none of us would like but might allow us all to walk away from this without anyone else getting hurt."

"Like I said, we don't negotiate."

Johnny pressed the talk key once more. "Then Tessa's head will be next."

"Don't you touch her!"

"Would you rather we send Scotty's head over?"

"You're supposed to be the law. How can you consider killing a woman?"

"From what I can tell, she walked in here as freely as any of the others. If she was acting under duress, she hasn't communicated that to any of my deputies."

"If you hurt Tessa, we'll storm that place!"

"Okay. You do what you have to do, and we'll do what we have to." Johnny turned the radio off.

Julianna turned off the recording device and handed it to Shane. "Sounds like we struck a nerve."

Shane placed the recorder in his pocket and stood up. "Sounds like we might have identified a schism in leadership also. I'll go play this back for Scofield and see if he has a preference as to whether his head or Tessa's should be on the chopping block next."

"You're going to let him decide?" asked Jimmy.

Shane turned toward the door. "I'm going to find out if he likes Tessa as much as Bonus does."

"Do you need me to come with you?" Bobby asked.

Shane paused to look at the big man. "Why don't you go have a conversation with Snake and Coot? One at a time. See what they're willing to tell you about the relationship between Scotty, Bonus, and Tessa."

"Willing to tell me?" Bobby asked.

"Yeah, but feel free to be persuasive." Shane made his way back to the jail where Sabas and Butterbean escorted him to Scotty Scofield's solitary confinement cell.

"When are you going to let me out of here, pig?" Scofield shouted when Shane arrived.

Shane stood inches away from the bars of Scotty's cell. "I'm going to be honest with you. That's not looking like it's going to happen for you; at least not in the way that you're probably imagining." Shane played back the conversation on the recorder for Scofield to listen to.

The founder of the Iron Devils seemed to lose some of his spunk during the playback. "You're not going to kill anyone."

Shane took a deep breath. "We don't really have

any other leverage against your gang. And they've already threatened to start terrorizing our town. Besides being our only option, it's sort of a moral imperative as well."

Scofield's eyes shifted from Shane, to Butterbean, to Deputy Sabas. "No, I'm not buying it."

"I've come here as a courtesy. To let you decide if it should be you or Tessa who meets their maker next." Shane pointed to Butterbean and Sabas. "Will you gentlemen shackle the prisoner and escort him to the basement?"

Scofield seemed less sure of himself as the deputies placed the restraints on his ankles. "What is this? Some kind of theatrics designed to get me to cave?"

"Why would I want you to cave?" Shane asked while they pulled Scofield out of the cell. "You're not in charge of the gang. Bonus is running the show now."

"If you were going to shoot me, you'd have killed me in my cell."

"The basement is already a mess," said Shane. "Kinda like, if you've been skinning fish in the bathtub, wouldn't be no point in messing up the kitchen sink, too."

When they arrived in the basement, Scofield panicked. "What did you do in here?"

"Like I said." Shane kicked the headless corpse of Ox. "Skinning fish."

Scotty pleaded. "Don't kill me! Please!"

"So, you want us to kill Tessa next? It has to be somebody. Your gang isn't backing down unless we can break their will."

"You don't have to kill either one of us. I'll get the Iron Devils to back down."

Shane laughed. "You're not in control."

"Yes, I am!" Scotty countered. "They'll do what I tell them!"

"What are you going to say?"

"If I get them to leave town, will you let us go? Me and Tessa, I mean?"

"If they leave the county, I'll let you live. But you're a criminal. I'm not letting you go."

"No deal! I'd rather be dead! Just kill me then."

Shane pressed the talk key on his walkie. "Jimmy, have them go ahead and kill the girl."

"Wait!" said Scofield. "I'll tell them to pull back. But you can't keep me locked up for the rest of my life. You have to tell me when I'm getting out of here."

"Hold on," Shane said into the mic. "The commissioners are considering an ordinance that would allow you to be set free after twenty-five lashes."

"Lashes, are you kidding?"

"No, I'm not."

"Can you give me a minute?"

Shane glared. "Don't take too long. We have to have a solution within the hour." Shane motioned for Sabas and Butterbean to follow him out of the room. He closed the door and locked it. "Deputy Sabas, keep an eye on the room. If he gives you any trouble, shoot him. We can always work that into our plan."

Butterbean gave a contorted frown. "You're

gonna leave him in there with that dead body?"

Shane lifted his shoulders as he started back up the stairs. "It might help him reach the right conclusion."

Once back in the sheriff's office, Shane debriefed the others on how his encounter with Scofield had gone.

Next, Bobby filled them in on what he'd learned from his conversation with Coot. "The chubby one says that Tessa and Bonus used to be an item."

"Let me guess," said Julianna. "Scotty and Tessa hooked up once after a long night of drinking."

"Yeah," Bobby confirmed. "While she was still with Bonus."

"And they've had trouble in Camelot ever since," Jimmy added.

Johnny sat behind his desk with his hands folded. Finally, he looked up at Shane. "See if he'll take the deal. I'm sure if we set him free he'll be back, but it will buy us some time to get organized. Tell him he has to sit for one month before we turn him loose. Hopefully, that will keep the Iron Devils at bay long enough for us to get our act together."

"I think it's a good plan," Shane nodded.

"What about the rest of them?" Julianna asked. "Every person we set free is going to be another shooter in the next engagement."

Johnny stared at the wood grains in his desk. "I know, but we can't very well execute them for criminal mischief."

Shane countered, "We're pretty far beyond criminal mischief. At the very least, they're part of a conspiracy to commit murder, overthrow the local government, and enslave the town. We're going to have to kill these people. The only question is whether we're going to put a bullet in their heads while we have them in custody or set them free so they can go get a gun and take a few of us with them when they die."

The mayor and the sheriff looked at each other for a while but neither said anything.

"He's right," said Julianna. "If you let them go, it might be one of you that they kill next time around."

"Or worse," Shane said. "It could be one of your wives, children, or grandchildren."

"We can keep them locked up," said the sheriff.

"We have two days of food. You can't keep the prisoners that you have already," Shane argued.

"Go see what Scotty decided," said Johnny. "We'll figure everything else out later."

"Okay." Shane dismissed himself and returned to the basement.

Sabas opened the door for him. Shane walked in to see Scotty Scofield staring at the humongous headless corpse in the open body bag. "What did you decide?"

"I'll do it." Scofield's expression was anything but remorseful and anything but defeated.

"Good. Deputy Sabas, will you assist me in escorting Mr. Scofield up to the sheriff's office?"

"Absolutely." Sabas grabbed Scotty's arm, which was restrained behind his back. "Let's go."

Shane followed Sabas and Scotty up the stairs so he could keep an eye on the muscular biker. Even though he was restrained, he still might try something. If he did, Shane wouldn't hesitate to gun him down.

"Sheriff Teague, this is Scotty Scofield, the founder of the Iron Devils," Shane made the introductions.

"You came to the wrong town, Mr. Scofield. If we let you go, do I have your word that you'll never be back in Jackson County?" Johnny asked.

"When are you going to let me go?"

"In one month. Your gang is going to need a little cooling-off period."

"Will you let Tessa go?" Scofield asked. "When you let me go, I mean?"

"Are you renegotiating?" Shane took control of the conversation.

"I can't leave without her."

Shane crossed his arms. "Then you'll trade her for ten other members."

"No way!"

"If you want something from me, you'll have to give me something in return."

"Ten of my guys aren't going to voluntarily turn themselves in to the screws!"

"I didn't say they had to be alive," Shane replied. "Next month, we'll let you out, and then it's up to you how you serve up the members you want to trade for Tessa."

Scofield looked at the sheriff in unbelief. "Is this guy for real?"

Johnny stood up. "I'm going to dismiss myself from this line of negotiation, for obvious reasons. But know that Deputy Black has full authority to make deals on behalf of this office." He patted his brother on the shoulder. "Come on, Jimmy. You don't need to be around for this either. Bobby, you hang around for security."

Bobby nodded and closed the door behind Jimmy, Johnny, and Deputy Sabas.

"You staying?" Shane asked Julianna.

She lifted her shoulders. "I'm not trying to get re-elected for anything."

"Make it five," said Scotty.

Shane nodded. "Let me guess, Bonus will be among the dead."

"I didn't say dead. You did." Scotty shuffled his shackled feet. "But yeah, Bonus will probably be part of the deal."

"And he has a few guys that are loyal to him," Julianna sat with one leg up on Johnny's desk.

"I'm not discussing my business with you people. Do we have a deal or not?"

Shane held up the mic. "Start talking." He pressed the talk key.

"Bonus, pick up. This is Scotty."

"Scotty," Bonus replied. "How's it going in there?"

"Listen, they've agreed to let us go if you pull back. Have everyone mount up and ride out. I'll meet you in Deal's Gap next month."

"Scotty, you know I can't do that."

"Yes, you can. I'm ordering you to!"

"I'm in charge right now. You're incapacitated, and I'm next in line."

"I'm locked up! That's not incapacitated."

"You might be acting under duress. I'm sure they've threatened you. Maybe even tried to get to you through Tessa. We can't compromise the mission of the entire gang because you got locked up. We'll break them. And we'll get inside. When we do, we'll set you free and set up shop, just like we talked about. We're not going to abandon our entire long-term strategy over one little hiccup."

"Bonus! Listen here! You are going to do what I tell you to, or you'll pay for it when I get out."

"I don't think I will. I don't even think this is you talking. I mean, I recognize your voice and all, but this is the fear inside you. It's not what you really want. I'm going to turn off the radio now. I'll see you when we take the building. Sit tight."

"Bonus! Bonus! Don't turn off the radio!" Scotty Scofield screamed into the microphone.

"Sounds like you're not in charge anymore." Julianna crossed her arms.

"Who are you supposed to be?" Scotty turned to Shane. "What is she doing in here? What does she have to do with anything?"

"She's my top adviser, so you might not want to speak so disrespectfully to her. If this doesn't work out, she might be the one who tips the scales in one direction or the other."

"In favor of what?" asked Scotty.

"Your head staying on your shoulders," said Shane. "Let's take you up to the roof and give you a bullhorn. Maybe you can convince your gang to listen to you directly. Let them know that Bonus isn't following orders."

Scotty dropped his head. "It won't work."

"Don't you want to try?" Shane lifted his eyebrows. "Our options for making use of your captivity get precipitously lower if you can't make something happen for us. If even one of our people gets shot, I promise, you will die. So will Tessa."

"I understand you, but if you cart me up there on the roof with a bullhorn, they'll know I've caved." Scotty looked Shane in the eyes. "On the other hand, if you cut me loose, I can go out there and take charge. Send me out there with a gun, and I'll deliver Bonus to your front door."

"Forget it. That's not going to happen."

"Then I don't know what else I can do to help." Scotty shrugged.

"Take him back to his cage!" Shane pointed to the door.

"Come on." Bobby grabbed Scotty by the arm and hauled him away.

CHAPTER 6

Hell from beneath is moved for thee to meet thee at thy coming: it stirreth up the dead for thee, even all the chief ones of the earth; it hath raised up from their thrones all the kings of the nations. All they shall speak and say unto thee, Art thou also become weak as we? art thou become like unto us? Thy pomp is brought down to the grave, and the noise of thy viols: the worm is spread under thee, and the worms cover thee.

Isaiah 14:9-11

Shane sat across from the sheriff in his office. "I don't know what to do."

Johnny looked at his watch then turned to his brother. "Time's up. We have to deliver on our promise. Otherwise, we look weak and we have no credibility."

Jimmy crossed his arm and looked out through the glass wall at the deputies and volunteers standing guard. "If we kill Scotty or Tessa, we'll only enrage the Iron Devils. We're outnumbered and they know it."

Johnny looked at Shane. "I know you don't like it, but I think sending Scotty out there to take charge might be our best bet."

"He'll turn on us in a second. What about killing Coot or Snake, as a final warning?" Shane looked at each of the others in the room.

Julianna shook her head. "No. We said Scotty or Tessa. Shooting Coot or Snake will be seen as a half-action. We'll appear to be bluffing."

"Bobby, what do you say?" Shane inquired.

"I vote to kick him. Maybe Scotty gets out there and incites a civil war."

Dan leaned against the office wall. "If so, we can jump on the opportunity and snipe off as many as possible from the roof."

Shane considered the wisdom of setting Scotty loose. "Plus, we still have Tessa. I'm not sure he'd sacrifice himself for her, but he might back down if he thought we were going to kill her."

Johnny nodded. "Sounds like we have a decision. Shane and Bobby walk him out. Make sure he understands what is expected of him and remind him that it won't go well for Tessa if he doesn't get the Iron Devils out of the county by sunset."

"Do you want to give him a gun?" Julianna asked.

Johnny glanced at the mayor before answering. "Give him one of those little pea shooters that Coot and Snake came in with. No more than four rounds. That's all he needs to put down Bonus."

Shane and Bobby stopped by the evidence room to get a pistol for Scotty, then went to collect him from his cell.

When they arrived Shane banged on the door. "This is our final offer."

"I'm all ears," said Scofield.

"We're going to send you out there. You're going to serve up ten guys. Dead or alive, I don't care."

"The deal was five!"

"Five for Tessa; that was the deal. I want another five for you. I should ask for five more for sending you out there with a gun, but I'm feeling generous. Don't push it, though. This is a take-it-or-leave-it deal. You can say no, but I'm going to use Tessa as a human shield when we launch our assault from the rooftop. We'll cut down as many of your men as we can with the .50 cal and the snipers will take care of the rest. We'll string her up as cover for our snipers. Then, I'll stick her bloody corpse in here with you so the two of you can be together while you starve to death because there's no way I'm feeding you during this siege."

Scofield stood up from his rack. "Then let's do this thing."

Shane opened the door. "Don't look so dejected.

I'm sure you already know which other men you're going to kill besides Bonus. You've got your guys, and he's got his. Am I right?"

Scotty said nothing as they walked him to the door.

Deputy Thompson, the sheriff, Julianna, Dan, and the mayor were all waiting by the front door when they arrived. Shane unlocked Scotty Scofield's shackles and handed him the pistol.

"It's not loaded." Scofield looked at the empty magazine well beneath the handle.

"I'll slip you the mag when you're out the door. That way we can have the barricade back up by the time you have a round racked in the chamber." Shane pushed him toward the door as Bobby and Thompson moved the heavy metal desk. "Not that I don't trust you."

"Yeah, right." Scotty stepped out the door.

Shane tossed the magazine out behind him. "Close it up."

Bobby and Thompson returned the cumbersome desk to the doorway.

"Now we wait," said Julianna.

Shane nodded in agreement. "Now we wait."

Less than a minute passed before Shane heard the first gunshot. "I'm hoping that was Bonus."

"Unless Scofield is playing us," said Dan.

Julianna added, "Or unless Bonus got the jump on Scofield."

Shane pointed to the stairwell. "Let's go up to the second floor so we can get a better view."

The group followed Shane up to a narrow window where they could only see the two up-armored RVs parked in front of the building.

Ten minutes passed and they saw nothing. They heard nothing. Then, suddenly, a barrage of gunfire echoed from behind the pair of armored vehicles.

"Somebody is shooting at somebody!" Julianna held her rifle close as she peeked out the window toward the action.

Shane pressed his cheek against hers to vie for a glimpse of what was happening outside. The gunfire stopped and silence returned.

"Anything?" asked the sheriff.

"Nothing," replied Shane.

"Wait!" Julianna's voice was excited. "Someone is dragging a body out from behind the vehicle."

"I don't recognize him." Shane watched a thin young man being dragged by his heels. Blood stained the pavement in his wake.

Bobby stepped closer and was able to look over Shane and Julianna's heads. "Here comes another one."

Shane saw a bearded man who'd been shot point-blank in the face. "That's going to be a closed casket."

One after the other, bodies were piled up. "I still don't see Bonus," Julianna said.

"He could have figured out what was going down," said the mayor. "Maybe he beat Scotty to the draw."

"And he's taunting us by pulling out Scotty's supporters." Shane watched with great anticipation. "That's already sixteen bodies. Scotty didn't even want to kill ten. Something isn't right."

Johnny pushed the talk key on his walkie talkie.

"Everyone, be ready. We may be in for a fight!"

Shane began looking around. "We'll need half of our people on the first floor to keep the building from being breached and the other half on the roof to snipe the attackers. My team will take the roof if something pops off."

Johnny patted him on the back. "You guys take the .50 cal. You've only got three boxes of ammo, so make them count."

"We'll rip up that RV, for one thing. Bobby, you run the gun. Dan will reload. Julianna and I will provide cover fire." Shane sighed. "This is going to be a mess."

"Wait!" exclaimed Julianna. "They're bringing out another body!"

A hopeful smile came across Shane's face when he saw the bald-headed man with blood smeared across his face and handlebar mustache. "That's Bonus!"

"Still, we don't know that Scotty survived," said Jimmy. "It could be another one of the Iron Devils in charge."

"I don't think so," Shane rebutted. "How would they know to drag the bodies out for display?"

"Only one way to find out." Johnny keyed in the frequency for the Iron Devils. "Scotty Scofield, this is Sheriff Teague. Can you hear me?"

"This is Scotty. I want to talk to the guitar player."

Johnny passed the radio to Shane. "You're up."

"Go ahead for Deputy Black."

"I lived up to my end of the bargain. I even threw in a couple of freebies—for the gun I guess."

"Yeah, I see. How did you manage to pull that off?"

"We had a shootout. Those are some of my boys out there. This isn't a pleasant thing for me, so let's get on with it. Now it's your turn to fulfill your end. Send out Tessa, Coot, and Snake."

"Wait a minute," Shane protested. "We never said anything about Snake and Coot. As for Tessa, we'll let her go in one month. Same deal as we had for you originally."

"You never said nothing about a month! I'm not leaving here without my people."

"Then I guess all that killing was for nothing," Shane replied.

"Oh, it wasn't for nothing. I got my gang back. And if I don't have Snake, Coot, and Tessa out here in fifteen minutes, I'm sending them in there with orders not to come back out until they have your head on a pike! Don't think I'm above sacrificing a few for the sake of the many, either. I think I've proven myself as far as that concept is concerned."

Shane looked at Julianna, then the sheriff. "We're in a jam here."

Johnny looked at his brother, then back to Shane. "What do we do?"

"Send out Coot and Snake," Shane said.

"You're going to let them go?" Julianna's eyebrows snapped together.

"Yeah, then gun them down as soon as they step outside," Shane answered. "Maybe Scofield will reconsider whether or not he still wants us to send Tessa out after that."

"We need some time to think this over." Jimmy

pressed his lips together.

Shane pressed the talk key. "Give me a half-hour to talk it over with the sheriff."

"You mean give you a half-hour to get ready for me to storm the castle," said Scotty. "No way Jose'. You've got five minutes to pull them out of the cell. If they aren't out here by then, we're coming in."

Shane looked at the mayor and the sheriff. "What do you think?"

"I guess we have no choice," said the sheriff. "Shane, do what you have to do then prepare for an assault from the rooftop. I'll send you as many men as I can. I'll start getting the rest of them ready to hold the first level."

Shane pressed the talk key. "Okay, Scotty. You win. I'll have them out in five."

"Julianna, Dan, head up top. Bobby and I will meet you there shortly." Shane led the way to the jail.

Once there, Shane said to Butterbean, "We need Snake and Coot."

"For what?" he asked.

"We're cutting a deal with the Iron Devils. To get them to leave." Shane hated to mislead Butterbean, but he couldn't risk Snake and Coot overhearing his conversation. "I'll need you to stand guard at Tessa's cell. If we get double-crossed and Scofield tries to breach the sheriff's department, I need you to put her down then get out front and help us fight. Do you think you can do that?"

"Shoot an unarmed woman? Point blank?"

"If you don't, she'll be part of the gang responsible for torturing and enslaving Jackson

County long after we're all dead."

Butterbean swallowed hard. "I guess."

Shane looked deep into his eyes. "Don't guess, Butterbean. I need you to do this."

He kept his eyes low as he glanced up at Shane, then lowered his gaze to the keys in his hand. "Okay. I will."

Shane kicked the cell door where Snake and Coot were being held. "Come on, get up."

"What's going on?" asked Snake.

"You're out of here. Scofield has negotiated for your release. But he's not giving me much time, so I need you both to move fast and get your filthy biker clothes back on. If he tries to breach the compound before I can get you out there, I'll kill both of you in your tracks."

The two normally-sluggish bikers moved quickly after Shane's warning. Coot hurried out of the cell. "We're coming."

Snake looked hopefully at his robust comrade. "I told you Scotty would figure something out."

The two men rushed to put on their dirty jeans, boots, and Iron Devils jackets.

"Let's move!" Shane pointed toward the front of the building. "I want you two out of here even more than you want to leave."

"I don't know about that, boss!" Coot broke into a sprint.

When they arrived at the front door, Deputy Thompson and another volunteer removed the heavy desk which blocked the entrance. Shane removed the handcuffs from the two bikers while Bobby opened the door.

The two bikers whooped in celebration of their perceived good fortune. They scampered out the door like a pair of students on the last day of school. Shane drew his pistol and shot Snake in the back of the head. Coot turned and froze, staring at Shane with wide knowing eyes. Shane pulled the trigger once more and the hefty biker dropped dead next to his lanky accomplice.

Shane jerked the door closed. "Get that barricade back up! Bobby, let's go. We need to get to the roof."

Shane led the way up the stairs. He selected the frequency for Scotty Scofield on the radio. "I need another minute to get Tessa out of her cell. She's in a separate block, but don't worry, she'll be out there next to Coot and Snake before you can grease your motorcycle chain."

"Wait!" screamed Scofield. "Don't you dare hurt her!"

"Or what?" Shane tried to hide his heavy breathing as he bounded up the stairs two at a time. "You've already said you're coming in here to kill us all. If Tessa is dead, that's one less Iron Devil I'll have to worry about once the shooting starts."

"Hang on, let's talk this over."

Shane reached the landing to the roof access. "Negotiation time is over. There's no way I'm going to give her to you alive and trust you'll move out once you have her. Unless you're willing to pull out and let me bring her to you in a month, I have nothing else to say."

Shane and Bobby stepped out onto the roof. Bobby took his position behind the .50 cal. Dan sat next to an open box of ammunition. Shane knelt next to Julianna with his rifle ready to fire. The radio was silent. The seconds ticked by like a three-legged turtle.

"What do you think he's going to do?" Julianna asked.

Shane shook his head. "I don't even think he knows."

Finally, Scofield called back. "One month, no lashes, no further retribution. You'll keep her in her own cell and feed her good food. And I want to talk to her on the radio every Sunday."

Shane looked at Julianna.

"That's as close to capitulation as you're going to get. You better take it," Julianna said.

Shane let the barrel of his rifle rest on the ledge of the roof. He picked up the radio. "This ain't the Ritz. We're all living off of scraps. I'll make sure she eats twice a day, but I can't make any promises about the quality of her meals. I don't have any problem with you speaking to her on Sundays but no questions trying to get intelligence about the jail, personnel, or the town. Calls will be limited to five minutes."

Scofield replied, "You'll bring her to the county line on US-74. The section that goes over the river. You'll park on one side of the bridge, and I'll park on the other. Then you'll send her across. Thirty days from today. August 12th at noon."

"The 12th?" Shane said. "Today's the 15th. Thirty days brings us to the 14th."

"You're not counting today."

"Today's over."

"Not yet."

"Still, that brings us to the 13th."

"My crew doesn't like to commit to anything on the 13th. Call us superstitious."

"Then I'll bring her on the 14th."

Agitation could be heard in Scofield's voice. "You'll bring her on the 12th , or we'll be rolling right back into your little town on the 13th."

"I thought you didn't like to commit to anything on the 13th; being superstitious and all."

"We'll make an exception."

"Fine," Shane agreed. "I'll bring her to you at noon on the 12th. After that, the Iron Devils will never come close to Jackson County."

"Deal. One more thing."

"No more things!" Shane snapped. "We're done here. Pack it up and roll out."

"No! You're going to grant me this last request, or we ain't going anywhere. I want to talk to her before we go. Let her know that everything is going to be okay."

Shane looked at Julianna who nodded. He got up from his position and made his way to the stairs. "Five minutes. Same rules as I mentioned before. Don't try to get any information from her. I'll be listening."

Shane hustled down the stairwell and made his way to the jail. He walked up to Tessa's cell where Butterbean sat, guarding her faithfully. "Someone wants to talk to you." Shane kept control of the radio and pressed the talk key for her.

"Hello?" she said.

"Hey baby, I'm going to get you out of there."

"Scotty? How did you get out?"

"It's a long story. They're going to bring you to me on August 12th. Don't worry. They'll do it. Because they know if they don't that the big bad wolf is going to blow their house down."

"Where are you going to go?" she asked.

"I can't tell you that, but we won't be far. They're gonna feed you right, and I'm gonna call on the radio every Sunday. I love you, baby."

"Then don't leave me here!"

"I ain't got no choice, baby. They shot Coot and Snake point blank in cold blood. They was going to do the same to you. This is the best we can do—for now. I'll talk to you next Sunday, and I'll see you in a month."

Her voice sounded dejected. "Okay. See you then."

Shane exchanged nasty looks with the prisoner and walked away. He hurried back to the rooftop to see if the Iron Devils were pulling back. "What's happening?"

Julianna peeked over the ledge. "Some of the bikers near the back are starting their engines."

Shane had to remind himself to breathe as he waited for the armored RV's to move. But eventually, he saw them start their engines and drive out of the parking lot.

Dan and Bobby slapped each other's palms together in a high-five gesture of victory. The other deputies and volunteers on the roof began clapping.

Julianna embraced Shane. "You did it!"

He cherished the closeness. "We did it!"

She pulled away and looked as if she were going

to kiss him. He considered closing the gap but had been burnt for such a thought not so long ago. He was sure he saw her lips begin to pucker, but the kiss never came.

Instead, she said, "Do you think they'll honor their commitment not to come back?"

Shane sat down with his back against the ledge of the roof. "No. In fact, I'm sure of it."

"How so?"

"Something he said to Tessa. He said *that's the best we can do—for now*. A little pause before *for now* was to let her know that he'd take revenge on us for keeping her locked up." Shane relished the temporary victory, knowing it would be short-lived.

"When do you think they'll hit us?"

"As soon as she crosses the bridge. I think he'll have an ambush waiting for whoever delivers Tessa, then the rest of them will be ready to take the town by surprise."

"I guess we have a month to get ready for it." Julianna sat next to him.

Shane sat pensively. "Twenty-seven days."

"Now what?" she asked.

"We'll give them an hour or so to clear out, then we'll go home and see Cole. Tomorrow morning, we'll wake up and figure out how we're going to fight back against an overwhelming force. We have to come up with a way to strike down the Iron Devils—once and for all."

She put her head on his shoulder. "I like that plan."

CHAPTER 7

In thee, O Lord, do I put my trust; let me never be ashamed: deliver me in thy righteousness. Bow down thine ear to me; deliver me speedily: be thou my strong rock, for an house of defence to save me. For thou art my rock and my fortress; therefore for thy name's sake lead me, and guide me. Pull me out of the net that they have laid privily for me: for thou art my strength. Into thine hand I commit my spirit: thou hast redeemed me, O Lord God of truth.

Psalm 31:1-5

Shane jumped at the sound of someone banging

on the front door of his trailer. He threw back the sheet and bounded from his bed, grabbing his pistol on the way to the door. Shane looked out the window to see Julianna's red ponytail. He opened the door with the pistol pointed at the floor. "What's the matter?"

She looked at his boxer shorts, then his legs. Her eyes traced up his bare torso to his eyes. She ran her hands over her thin green dress as if smoothing out wrinkles which weren't there. "It's Sunday. You're supposed to be helping me lead worship, then you're supposed to preach."

Shane put his palm on his forehead. "Sunday. I completely lost track of what day it is."

"Considering what we went through yesterday, I think most people will understand. But hurry."

"I will." He turned to go back inside.

She caught the door before he could shut it. Her eyes glanced at his legs and chest once more. "And don't forget your guitar!"

"Right." He hurried off to get ready.

***

After service Sunday afternoon, the 20 or so members of the Teague family hung around the Black compound for a potluck lunch, which had become the custom. George and Carrol Franz also stayed.

Carrol patted Shane on the back. "That was a wonderfully inspirational message you gave this morning. I'll admit, I was a tiny bit apprehensive that you wouldn't have anything prepared, considering what you had to endure at the sheriff's department over the weekend. Then, when you were late, I was sure of it. Boy was I wrong. Not that we wouldn't have understood if you hadn't been able to put a message together. What I'm trying to say is, your father and mother would be proud."

"Thanks." Shane hugged her.

Julianna stood nearby. She waited for Carrol Franz to walk off. "How did you manage to pull that sermon together? You obviously weren't writing a Bible study this morning."

"I don't know. I opened Pastor Joel's Bible to Psalms and that one was staring at me. Then Pastor Joel had a bunch of notes scribbled in the margin. It all sort of fell together."

"Almost like God took pity on you and bailed you out."

Shane laughed. "Yeah, almost."

"You better get in line if you want any of Mrs. Betty's chicken. It's always the first thing to go."

Shane watched Cole running and playing with Scott Ensley and several of the Teague children. "I'm feeling pretty blessed right now, even if I miss out on the fried chicken."

"Me too, but we don't have to miss out if we get in line." She took his hand and led him to the queue. "Jimmy and Johnny are going to want to talk about the Iron Devils after lunch."

"I know."

"Any thoughts?"

"When Scotty was trying to get Bonus to pull back he said he'd meet them in Deal's Gap. I wonder if that's where they're going to hide out while they're waiting for Tessa to serve out her time."

"Could be. It's a big biker hang out."

"Oh yeah?"

"That section of US 129 is called the Tail of the Dragon. It has the most turns of any comparable length of road in the country. It's about 11 miles long. I suppose it's a challenge to drive, especially on a bike."

Shane thought for a moment. "Maybe we should go stake it out. If they camp out there, we could mobilize everyone in town that's able to pull a trigger and hit them while they're asleep."

"You make it sound so easy." Julianna picked up a plate. "First off, how are we going to stake out a biker spot? We'll stick out like a beetle in a bag of rice."

"We could pose as bikers." Shane spooned a generous portion of green beans onto his plate.

"Pose as bikers. How do you suggest we do that?"

"We have Snake and Coot's bikes. Plus the bikes left behind by the other Iron Devils killed in the Bonus and Scotty skirmish."

"Most of the bikes left behind were the wrecked ones which got all messed up driving over the road spikes. Anyway, you don't think Scotty would recognize Coot and Snake's bikes sitting in a parking lot?"

"A few flat tires on the wrecked bikes, but otherwise, a lot of good parts." Shane was pleased to see a few chicken legs remaining in the pan. "Maybe we could trade for some different bikes."

"Sounds like a sketchy plan." Julianna took a piece of breast.

Shane led the way to a table where Jimmy was waving to him. The table was an old door propped up on sawhorses with sections of logs all around, which served for chairs.

"We saved you a seat," Johnny Teague said.

Julianna sat next to Shane. "Just wait until you fellows hear what he has cooked up now."

Shane explained the bare-bones plan for scouting out the Iron Devils' location, then hitting them with a sneak attack.

Dan said, "I know some boys who ride. They live up in Maggie Valley. Couple of them work on bikes. Of course, that was all before the world went to pot. If they're still around, they'd be your best bet for swapping out those other bikes."

"They don't happen to belong to a gang, do they?" Julianna asked.

"Not a one-percenter gang, but they've got a little club called the Hill Runners."

"One-percenters?" Shane questioned. "What are you talking about? Like ultra-rich motorcyclists?"

"No," Dan laughed. "Some fella from some big motorcycle association said ninety-nine percent of all bikers are law-abiding citizens. One-percenters are those who consider themselves to be criminals."

"Oh, like the Iron Devils," said Shane.

Dan answered, "That'd be one example, sure."

"Do you think they'd consider making us honorary members? Long enough for us to wear their patch and do our little recon mission?" Julianna pulled the chicken meat away from the bone with her fork.

"Normally, no," Dan replied. "But times being what they are, we're all willing to bend the rules a little, especially for a price."

"Think you can ride up there with us tomorrow and make some introductions?" Shane inquired.

Dan finished chewing, then wiped his mouth. "I can't make any promises, but we can take a trip up there."

"Scotty Scofield has seen your faces. Even if you manage to swap out the bikes, he'll recognize both of you, especially if you're together." Jimmy sopped his plate with a piece of cornbread.

"Maybe not," said Julianna. "I could dye my hair black. I'd look dramatically different."

Johnny set his fork on the table. "Shane, you've got a beard started from not shaving since the Iron Devils showed up. You could let it keep growing and shave your head."

"Shave his head?" Julianna protested. "That would be a crime!"

"It'll grow back," Johnny said. "Besides, what difference does it make to you?"

"I'm allowed to have an opinion, aren't I?" She pointed to the dogwood by the drive. "I'd hate to see that tree cut down, but that doesn't necessarily mean I've got a thing for it."

"No," Johnny smiled. "Not necessarily."

"It's my hair," said Shane. "I'll shave it."

Julianna looked at his thick black hair and sighed. "I suppose it's for a good cause."

***

Monday morning, Shane and Dan rolled the damaged Harley Davidson up the simple wooden ramp into the back of the Dodge mega-cab. They repeated the process for another wrecked bike which had been sitting in the parking lot of the Jackson County Sheriff's Department since the siege. Shane shut the tailgate. "Julianna, take it easy with the truck. I've never ridden a motorcycle before."

"It's just like a bicycle, only faster." Dan laughed as he stepped on to Coot's Harley. He walked Shane through the basics of starting and shifting. "Think you got all that?"

"Better let me take a few laps around the parking lot before we get on the road." Shane started Snake's Harley and rode at low speed around the sheriff's department complex.

"I think you've got it!" Julianna yelled.

"I hope so." Shane pulled up next to the truck and cut the engine. "Dan and I only have pistols. All the big guns are in the Ram."

"At least I'll be safe." She winked at him.

"Yeah, but seriously, stay close." Shane started the engine once more.

"Let's ride!" Dan led the way out of the parking lot.

Shane soon got the hang of riding on the open road, and the short trip lasted only half an hour.

Dan pulled off the main road and onto a side street, which was a little more challenging for Shane than the highway had been. The ride ended at a huge four-car metal garage situated on a wooded

Gehenna

lot behind a small single-wide trailer.

Dan cut the engine to his bike as did Shane. Julianna parked behind them and exited the truck. "Looks like he has his priorities straight."

"Yep, he spends all his time in that garage. Just goes to the trailer to sleep. And I'm not so sure about that." Dan walked toward the garage.

An older biker with long gray hair and short gray beard came out front.

"Bunny." Dan waved. "Is Wrench around?"

"He's in there." Bunny looked over the bikes. "When did you start riding?"

"Always wanted to. Finally made the time for it." Dan continued walking toward the garage.

"Harley Softail, that's a heck of a first bike. Must have got that before the crash."

"Actually just picked it up this morning."

"You must be doing better than most then."

Dan laughed. "Not exactly. Let's find Wrench, and I'll tell you all about it."

Once inside the garage, another old biker came out from behind a partially disassembled motorcycle. Wrench had thinning black hair, thick glasses, and a handlebar mustache. He wiped his greasy hand on the front of his coveralls and offered it to Dan. "Good to see you."

Dan shook his hand and introduced Shane and Julianna.

"Oh, yeah! You're that guitar player! Boy! She's prettier than that little blonde one you got engaged to in New York City. Whatever happened to her?" Wrench looked at Julianna like it had been a while since he'd seen a real woman.

85

"She was killed—shortly after New Year's."

"Oh." Wrench looked at the oily concrete floor of his garage. "I'm sorry. I didn't know."

"It's okay." He looked at Julianna. She looked annoyed. Probably over being spoken of as though she weren't in the room, or perhaps over the insinuation that she was Shane's new little plaything which had replaced the *blonde one*.

"I've got some bikes that I thought you might be interested in," said Dan.

"I might be interested, but I don't know what I could give you for them. In case you haven't noticed, we're going through some hard times."

"How about different bikes?" Dan looked around at the various works in progress. "We need three good bikes. I've got four to trade."

"Let's see what you've got," said Wrench.

Dan pointed to the bikes he and Shane had ridden up from Sylva. "These two are in great condition. The two in the back of the truck have a couple of scratches and might need new tires. But nothing you can't handle."

Wrench and Bunny checked out the two Softails. "Fine machines, both of them," Bunny commented.

"Yep. May I ask how you came to acquire them?" Wrench looked up at Dan.

Dan provided a brief narrative of the conflict in Sylva.

"Iron Devils." Wrench ran his greasy fingers through his thinning hair. "They came through here a while back. Haywood County put up a show of force. I think the gang was staking out the area but decided to move on. I guess I could swap out some bikes for these. Might not be in this good of a condition."

"That's alright. We just need something to make us blend in." Shane looked around at the bikes in the yard. "But we need Harleys or some other kind of serious bikes. A Gold Wing isn't going to produce the desired effect."

Julianna put her indignation aside and took on a more charming aura. "What would it take to become honorary members of your motorcycle club?"

Bunny seemed unwilling to deny her request. "That's not something we normally do, but we might be able to make an exception for you, darlin'."

"What about for all of us?" Dan inquired.

"That's a little bit bigger favor, now." Bunny's thick gray eyebrows dipped low on his forehead.

Shane made his opening offer. "Would fifty gallons of gas help grease the gears?"

"Fifty gallons?" Wrench looked at Bunny with excitement.

Bunny smiled. "I think it might."

"Any chance you boys would want to take a ride with us?" Dan asked.

"Where to?" Wrench inquired.

Dan replied, "Dell's Gap."

"If it's to tangle with the Iron Devils, probably not," said Bunny.

"This is just to confirm their locations. We don't even want to make eye contact. I can offer you a couple more lightly used bikes for your trouble," said Shane.

"What kind of bikes?"

"Harleys. Similar to the others. They might need a little paint, a new headlight, and a set of tires. But like Dan said, you can handle that." Shane waited for the reply.

The two bikers looked at each other. Wrench turned back to Shane. "I believe we can accommodate your request."

"Good, can you have the bikes ready to roll tomorrow morning?" Shane began walking toward the truck.

Wrench lowered his brows. "I've got so many different projects going right now."

"You just need to focus on having three bikes ready." Dan patted him on the back. "Leave everything else until you get back."

"I could be ready to roll out Wednesday morning." Wrench walked alongside Shane and the others.

"That will work." Dan pointed to Bunny. "Keep him on task. Don't let him wander off to some other project. Pick out the bikes and make sure he sticks with them. Can you have us some jackets with patches by Wednesday?"

"You didn't say anything about jackets," Bunny replied.

"What do you need to make that happen for us?" Shane paused from walking.

"Guns," said Bunny.

"How about we throw in some small-caliber pistols?" Shane asked.

"I had something a little bigger in mind. How about some AR-15s, magazines, and 500 rounds of ammo?"

Shane shook his head. "No way. We don't need fancy leather jackets. In fact, we could roll with denim vests, as long as they have a patch on the back. I'll give you one AR, two mags, and 100 rounds of ammo, which is already way too much for three vests. But this mission is important to us."

Bunny shook his hand to seal the deal. "See y'all soon."

"See you then." Shane led the way back to the truck.

"What about Bobby?" Julianna asked. "Shouldn't we get a vest and a bike for him?"

"No," said Shane. "Scofield has seen him. Bobby's size is going to stick out no matter what disguise you put him in. He'll bring too much attention to us."

CHAPTER 8

All warfare is based on deception.

Sun Tsu

Shane knocked on the door of the guest cabin Wednesday morning. Cole came to the door. "Mama!" His voice sounded distressed.

"Hey, buddy. It's me. I just got a haircut. That's all." Shane felt sorry for upsetting his son by showing up bald but couldn't help but be a little amused by the situation.

Julianna came to the door and stared at Shane's head. She knelt down and hugged Cole. "It's okay, sweetie. Mama is scared, too. It's not the kind of thing anyone should have to look at, especially a little boy. Hopefully, he'll let it grow back as soon as we return."

Cole turned and buried his face in his mother's shoulder. "When are you coming back?"

"Tomorrow or the next day. You be good for Aunt Angela." She hugged him and kissed him.

"Will your hair still be black?" he asked.

"Not for long, baby. This is just a costume." She kissed him once more and stood up.

Shane bent down to hug his son. "I love you, buddy. We'll see you soon."

Cole warmed and put his hands around his neck. "I love you, too, Shane."

Shane stood up and waved to his sister who had come to the door. "We'll see you in a couple of days."

"Be safe." Angela hugged him.

"We will." Shane led the way to the truck where Dan was already waiting in the back seat. Two more wrecked bikes were in the bed of the vehicle as well as several containers of gasoline. Julianna rode shotgun while Shane drove.

Shane stopped at the end of the gravel drive to wait for Bobby to open the front gate. Shane rolled down the window. "Make sure everyone is ready to roll out with a one-hour notice. As soon as we confirm that Scofield is there, we'll return. I don't want to give them a chance to slip away."

"You got it." Bobby's large hand held the corner of the gate. "I'll hold down the fort while you're gone."

"I know you will." Shane waved as he pulled through the open gate. "I appreciate it."

Thirty minutes later, they arrived at Wrench's garage. Shane, Julianna, and Dan exited the Ram.

Dan waved at Bunny. "We brought your gas, but we'll need to take the containers with us when we leave."

"Sure, I've got plenty of empty gas cans." Bunny smiled at Julianna. "I like them boots. Wait until you see the jacket I found for you." He turned to go inside the garage.

Shane said, "I think Bunny is sweet on you. If you want, I could tell him that you're my old lady."

"As tempting as that sounds, I'll take my chances with Bunny and Wrench." She frowned in anticipation of her new Hill Runners jacket.

Wrench came out wiping his hands on a dirty towel. "Hey!"

Shane felt worried. "We're ready to roll, aren't we?"

"Oh, sure. Just making a few last-minute adjustments." Wrench turned to go back inside. "Come on. I'll show you what we've got for you."

The three of them followed the old biker inside. Wrench handed a key to Dan. "This here is a 2004 Panhead. I've been meanin' to give her a fresh coat of paint, but never got around to it."

"That will work." Dan got on and fired up the engine.

Wrench handed another key to Shane. He yelled to be heard over Dan's bike. "This black one is a 99 Fat Boy. The chrome is a little pitted in places, but the bike purrs like a kitten."

Dan cut the engine and walked over to inspect Shane's bike.

"Finally, I got somethin' special for the lady." Wrench handed Julianna a key. "This red one is a customized 2014 Indian Scout."

"Wow!" Julianna seemed to genuinely like the shiny red bike.

Bunny returned with a leather jacket for her. "Put this on before you sit on it."

"Thanks." She slipped on the sleek black biker jacket, then got on the motorcycle.

Bunny handed Shane and Dan denim jackets with the Hill Runners patch on the back.

Wrench walked Julianna through the functions of the bike. "Think you can handle it?"

"My cousin had a dirt bike when we were kids. It's been a while, but I think it'll come back to me."

Shane interrupted Bunny and Wrench who appeared to be getting such a thrill from turning Julianna into a biker chick. "We need to get this show on the road."

"Yeah, okay," said Bunny. "Let me load up my saddlebags."

"Want me and Bunny to take the lead?" Wrench offered.

"Do you know the way?" Shane asked.

"Oh yeah. We've been out there many times. I know the owner of the hotel."

"Great. We'll follow. Keep in mind that we're not used to curves, so keep it slow." Shane slipped on his jacket. His bike had no cargo space so he packed his essentials into one of Julianna's saddlebags, then mounted his motorcycle.

The five of them were soon on the road. The trip ordinarily would take only an hour and a half, but Wrench and Bunny made allowances for the neophyte riders, and they arrived two hours after leaving Maggie Valley.

Shane pulled up to the gas pumps, which all had *Out of Order* signs posted. He cut his engine as did the others.

"Looks like your hunch was right." Julianna pointed at the rows of motorcycles parked in front of the long, single-story motel building.

Dan pointed at two bikers walking across the road to the bar on the opposite side. "Those look like Iron Devils patches."

"Yep," said Wrench.

"Where's the office?" Shane asked.

"In the store." Bunny stepped off his bike. "Come on. I'll show you."

"The rest of you stay out here and keep an eye on the bikes." Shane followed Bunny. Once inside, he looked at a large sheet of poster board, which had various exchange rates hand-written with black marker. He made a mental note of the items the resort accepted as currency. "Gold, booze, cigarettes, gas, silver, ammo."

"Good morning." A tall slender man with round-rim glasses and a black leather vest called out to Shane and Bunny from behind the desk.

"Good morning to you," said Bunny. "How much for two rooms?"

"Ain't got no rooms," said the man.

"Got any opening up after checkout time?" Bunny asked.

"Nope. Got a whole club stayin' here for a while. They're already on the list for anything that opens up. Robbinsville still has a motel or two open for business."

Bunny laughed. "Rest of the country is shuttered-up like a ghost town, but most all the biker businesses are still putterin' right along."

"Our people are a little more—resourceful, I guess. Y'all run some kinda shop?"

"Yeah, I handle the office for a garage over in Maggie. We've been through here a few times."

The man pushed his glasses up on his nose. "Oh, yeah. I thought you looked familiar."

"Don't reckon you could do us a favor seein' how we're locals, do you?"

"Fraid not." The man shook his head.

"Is that your place up top?" Shane pointed toward the ceiling. "I noticed some kind of apartment up over the store."

"Yeah, but I ain't got no extra room."

Shane placed a 20-franc French gold rooster on the counter. "Would we be able to convince you to take a room over in Robbinsville? We'd make it worth your while."

The clerk picked up the coin. "90 percent?"

"Yeah. Just under a fifth ounce of gold." Shane watched the man's eyes.

The man looked back up at Shane. "For how long?"

"Two nights."

"Why would you pay so much for a one-bedroom apartment?"

"I'm willing to pay a premium to not have to answer a lot of questions and to be where I want to be."

The man stuck the coin in his pocket. "Fair enough. Discretion has always been one of the big draws for our little resort. I'll just need to pack a few things. You can have it in about an hour."

"That will be fine." Shane looked over the sparsely stocked shelves. The small store had few commodities, and the ones which were available were astronomically priced.

"Wooster ought to be here shortly to open up the restaurant," said the clerk.

"What do you serve?"

"Depends on what Wooster can find. Venison, beans, and rice mostly. Might get some beef from time to time."

"Thanks." Shane wandered away from the counter.

On the way out, he overheard the clerk on his walkie talkie. "Tawny," the man called. "I need you to watch the counter for a while. We're going to stay at Dragon's Rest for a couple of days."

Shane walked back outside to inform the others of the arrangement. "We'll be able to keep an eye on all the comings and goings from the apartment. Dan, Julianna, and I will stay indoors as much as possible. We'll send Wrench and Bunny out if we need to get a closer look at anyone."

Bunny pointed at the old man opening the door to the restaurant. "Looks like Wooster is here. Maybe we should go inside where we'll be less visible."

Shane watched two more Iron Devils come out one of the motel rooms further down. "Good idea."

The group parked their bikes on the side of the store and walked to the simple dining room.

"Won't have nothin' to eat for a half an hour or

so, but y'all make yourselves comfortable if you want." The old man didn't stop working to address Shane's group.

"Don't rush on our account, old-timer," Wrench called back. "We ain't in no hurry."

Shane sat on one of the bar stools which looked out at the road and the parking lot. He studied the parking lot in front of the motel rooms.

"Do you see his bike anywhere?" Julianna pulled up a stool next to Shane.

"No, and it's not an easy one to miss. It's a custom chopper with white flaming skulls on maroon paint."

"Could be over at Dragon's Rest." Bunny sat on the stool next to Julianna.

Shane continued looking out the window. "If we haven't spotted Scofield by morning, maybe we'll split up. A couple of us can head over there."

Twenty minutes later, Wooster yelled, "Kitchen is open. Y'all come on."

Shane walked up to the counter. "What are you serving?"

"BBQ."

"BBQ what?"

"Venison. On white bread with baked beans."

"How much for five plates?"

"Ounce of silver."

"I don't have silver," said Shane.

"Exchange table is in the store," said Wooster. "But I'll take 25 rounds of 9mm if you got it. Otherwise, 15 rounds of .223 or 7.62."

"9mm will work." Shane looked at Dan. "Can you grab a box out of Julianna's saddlebag?"

"Be right back." Dan retrieved the ammunition out of the bike and returned to pay the old man. The group enjoyed a savory meal, then the store clerk came in to notify them that their room was ready.

Once inside, Bunny looked at Julianna. "What are the sleeping arrangements?"

Shane quickly answered, "Julianna will take the bedroom. The rest of us will share the living room. We'll flip a coin for the couch."

Julianna carried a small bag into the bedroom. "Shane, you can sleep in here with me."

"Oh," said Wrench. "I didn't realize you two were an item."

"We're not." Her eyes narrowed and turned to Shane. "On the floor, I mean."

Once everyone was settled into their space, Shane and Julianna watched the comings and goings of the bikers in the motel rooms while the others played cards to pass the time.

Shane said, "It seems they're getting more active as the day moves on."

Julianna nodded. "My guess is that they were up late last night partying. That looks like an operational still over behind that bar across the street."

Shane watched three bikers sharing a joint on the porch of the bar. "Yeah. Seems like this place is well supplied."

The hours ticked by but still, Shane and Julianna saw no sign of Scotty Scofield. Once the sun set, the Iron Devils began crawling out of the motel rooms like cockroaches. The bar across the road filled to capacity with patrons spilling out onto the porch and into the parking lot.

Julianna pointed to a muscular man with blonde hair crossing the road toward the bar. "Is that him?"

Shane was joined by everyone else in staring out the window at the man who bore a close resemblance to Scotty Scofield. "I can't be sure. It's too dark."

Dan looked at Wrench and Bunny. "You boys are on deck."

Bunny put his jacket on. "What are we looking for?"

"A patch on his jacket that says founder," Shane replied.

Wrench held out his hand. "We're going to need a little spending money."

Shane went to the bedroom to get the half-filled box of 9mm ammo. He came back and placed it in Wrench's hand. "This should buy you a couple of drinks."

"We'll be back." Bunny walked out and closed the door to the apartment.

Shane watched with great anticipation while the two seasoned bikers set out on their mission. Half an hour later, they returned smelling of moonshine.

"That's your guy." Bunny pointed to the bar. Scofield's muscular frame and blonde hair made him recognizable from a distance.

"I wonder where he's keeping his bike," Julianna said.

"Probably got it in the room with him," Wrench replied.

"We need to find out which room he's in." Shane stared down at the bar. "When we come back, it'll be after they're all drunk and passed out. I want to hit Scofield's room first. We can't let him get away."

"We might see him leave from here, but we can't be sure which room he goes to." Julianna looked toward the row of motel rooms.

"Unless someone was watchin' from the bar." Bunny stepped closer to the window.

"Are you volunteering?" Shane asked.

Bunny smiled. "Are you buyin'?"

Shane knew they'd be sloshed and could risk compromising the entire mission if he sent them back right away. "He just got there. Let's give him some time to stretch his legs. I'll send you fellows back in a couple of hours."

Later that night, Dan fell asleep on the couch while Julianna lay down in the bedroom. Wrench and Bunny continued their marathon of cards.

Shane waited patiently to finally see the first sign of the Iron Devils retiring after a long night of drinking. "3:00 AM. Bunny, Wrench, I think it might be time for you guys to get back to work."

The two of them stood up to stretch. "Gonna need some more spendin' money." Wrench held out his hand once more.

Shane gave him another 25 rounds of 9mm ammo. "Make it last."

"This is about 5 drinks with tip. It ain't gonna last too long." Wrench seemed to be hinting that he wanted more.

"Sip your drinks. Don't feel like you have to chug them. This isn't college." Shane offered him no more currency of any sort.

"All right. We'll be back." Wrench waited for Bunny to leave before closing the door behind them.

Julianna came into the living room. She whispered so not to wake Dan. "How's it going?"

"These people seem like they can go all night."

"Why don't you go close your eyes for an hour or two? I'll wake you if I see anything."

"You don't mind?"

"I wouldn't have offered if I did."

Shane nodded. "Yeah, okay. Wake me as soon as you see Scotty leave the bar. He's inside right now."

"Sure. Sleep tight."

Shane stretched out on the bed. He closed his eyes for a second, and he was out.

***

"Shane, wake up," Julianna said.

He was roused from a deep slumber by her voice. "What time is it?"

"5:00 AM. Scotty just left."

"Do you see Wrench and Bunny?" Shane stretched and got up from the bed.

"They're chatting up some rough looking gals."

"Oh boy, I hope they're staying on task." Shane walked to the window. "You're right. I can't see much in the dark, but I can tell those girls have seen better days."

Julianna pointed at the woman speaking to Wrench who wore a leather halter top which revealed her tattooed back. "I'd be curious to see what's painted on that one's back."

"Looks like a mural. To each their own, I guess." In the dim light, Shane could make out that she had a full-color tattoo covering her entire back. "Wrench and Bunny don't seem to be wrapping up the conversation. Maybe I better go down there."

"What if somebody recognizes you?"

"Scotty is the only one who's ever seen my face close up. Even if the Iron Devils were as sober as a bench of judges, I doubt any of them would recognize me with my new haircut."

"Don't remind me."

Shane donned his denim Hill Riders jacket. "I'll be right back."

"If you insist on going, get a look at that tattoo. It's killing me to know what she could possibly have scrawled all over her back like that."

"Yeah, it's sorta like a bad car wreck. You can't help but look." Shane closed the door to the small apartment and walked softly down the stairs.

He kept watch to see if Scotty would re-emerge while he made his way across the road to the bar. He caught up with Wrench and Bunny. "Hey, guys."

"Hey, sugar!" said the one with the leather halter top. "What's your name?"

"We call him Baldy," Wrench laughed.

"I can see why." She ran her fingers across Shane's clean-shaven head.

"He's got an old lady," said Bunny.

"She ain't here right now." The woman got close enough for Shane to smell her breath, which was permeated by cigarettes and alcohol.

He stepped back. "Yeah, but she's not far."

"Well." The woman's skin was dry and thin. "I don't want to get you in any trouble."

Shane pulled Bunny to the side. "Did you see where he went?"

"Yeah, 113."

"That seems appropriate." Shane nodded. "But I thought he said he was superstitious."

"We might be superstitious about Friday the 13th, but most bikers don't mind the number. M is the 13th letter of the alphabet." Slurred Bunny. "Lots of 'em have 13 on their patch."

"What does M stand for?"

"Some will tell you motorcycle. Others say marijuana." Bunny chuckled and turned back to his lady friend. "We'll be on up in a little while."

"Sure." Shane turned to walk back to the apartment. "I suppose beauty is in the eye of the beholder."

Once inside, Julianna closed the door. "Did you get it?"

"113."

"What's that?" she asked.

"Scofield's motel room." Shane wondered why he needed to provide clarification.

"Oh, good." She looked slightly guilty. "But, I meant the subject of the tattoo."

"Oh, I don't know. It was something like an eagle flying over a mountain. Like an airbrush painting on the side of a van from the 70s."

"How weird." She stared out the window.

"Do you want to go back to sleep?" he asked.

"I don't think I could. But you can if you want."

"I'm up now. Besides, my mind is spinning at a hundred miles an hour thinking about how we're going to hit the Iron Devils now that we know where Scofield is staying."

"I'll keep vigil with you. It won't hurt to know what time the hard-core partiers finally give up and hit the hay."

CHAPTER 9

Never put off until tomorrow what you can do today.

Benjamin Franklin

Shane chugged his coffee Friday afternoon.

"You still look frazzled from the trip." Bobby sat with him at the picnic table under the shade of the chestnut trees. "Maybe we should hold off until tomorrow."

"No. We can't risk letting Scofield slip away. We have to strike while the iron is hot."

"So, how many of these bikers are going to fight alongside us?"

"Bunny said he thinks about thirty or forty will come out."

"That helps to even up the numbers. I imagine

they aren't doing it out of the goodness of their hearts."

"I told them they can have all the bikes, plus we'll split the weapons and ammo down the middle."

"Isn't that going to make a lot of noise? Having all those motorcycles roaring up a little mountain road in the wee hours of the morning?"

"No. They'll be coming in trucks. The Hill Riders are planning to go home on the spoils of war."

"What about this poor guy that runs the place? His motel is going to be trashed."

"I don't have a lot of sympathy for him. He knows what kind of work his patrons do. He has no illusions about why they're thriving while the rest of the country is gasping for air to survive. He can patch the place up after we're done and keep on keeping on. Or, he can close up shop and retire. It's all the same to me."

Jimmy and Johnny Teague walked up the long gravel driveway of the Black compound.

"Good afternoon, Shane. Welcome home," said the mayor.

"Good afternoon, Mayor, Sheriff."

Johnny took a seat at the picnic table. "Pop and the women are going to hole up at his house while we're gone. Angela is welcome to stay with them. I'd imagine she'll be watching Cole if Julianna insists on coming."

"Oh, yeah. She insists," Shane replied. "I appreciate the offer. I'm sure she'll take you up on it."

Jimmy added, "If something goes wrong, the Iron Devils will go straight to the sheriff's department. It might be a more secure location, but it will be the first target for retribution. For that reason, I think the women and kids will be safer at our compound than there."

"I agree," said Shane. "How many people are coming with us?"

"Thirty-five," Johnny replied. "Plus ever how many of the Hill Runners decide to help us out. I'm leaving Butterbean and three other deputies at the jail. I wouldn't feel right with anything less."

"It's a good call." Shane stood up and stretched. "Mr. Mayor, you're sitting this one out, right?"

Jimmy lowered his brows. "I'd have never taken this job if I'd known I'd have to sit on the bench for the whole game."

"If things go wrong, the town needs leadership." Shane put his hand on Jimmy's shoulder.

"I know." Jimmy looked up. "I'll be at the sheriff's department with Butterbean. That way I won't feel completely useless."

"We should start getting our gear ready. I want to go over the attack plans in detail with everyone tonight. We can all rest up for a while and then review the operation right before we roll out."

"What time do you want to leave here?" Johnny asked.

"3:00 AM. Deal's Gap is an hour and a half from here. Anyone still up and partying at 4:30 is going to be sloshed and represent a minimal threat to our invasion."

***

Shane, Julianna, Dan, and Bobby rode in the lead vehicle of the convoy to Deal's Gap. Shane pulled to the side of the road and cut the ignition to the Ram. "This is it. The resort is right around that turn. We'll cut through the woods and hit room 113 from the back."

Shane looked at the long line of vehicles behind his. His fellow soldiers got out of their trucks quietly with weapons ready to fight. He waved for them to follow, then led the way to the assault.

Shane and his team cut off from the main group and headed into the forest. They arrived at their intended destination within minutes. Shane checked the back door. "It's locked."

"I got it." Dan pushed his rifle to the back and let it hang from the sling while he bent down and picked the lock. Shane held a small flashlight so Dan could see what he was doing.

Dan placed his tools back in his pocket and turned the knob. He looked up at Shane with a smile. "We're in," he whispered.

Shane held his rifle ready to fire and led the team inside.

"Rhonda, is that you?" Scotty Scofield's voice sounded groggy and drunk. "I told you we can't keep doing this. Tessa is going to find out and…" He switched on the bedside light and saw Shane standing over him with his gun drawn.

"Your secret is safe with me." Shane pulled the trigger and shot Scofield between the eyes. "Let's keep moving. Out the front door!"

Bobby opened the door. Shane left the room first with Julianna right behind him.

"Hey! Who's shooting guns at 4:30 in the mornin'? Some people are trying to sleep!" An older biker stuck his head out the door of the room next to Scofield's.

Julianna dispatched him without hesitation.

"They're figuring it out." Shane saw the bikers across the street at the bar begin to take notice. Some drew weapons just as the other soldiers from Sylva arrived on the scene. A firefight ensued.

"Stay focused." Shane led the way. "We have to clear all these rooms!" He saw Bunny and Wrench leading a breach team at the far end of the motel. He didn't have time to acknowledge them but was glad they'd come along.

Shane entered the room next door where Julianna had killed the old biker. Two more hostiles were just inside and had drawn their pistols. They fired at Shane. Bobby came in behind him and aided in the gunfight. The bikers shot wildly but neither Shane nor Bobby were struck. Julianna and Dan remained in the doorway and dropped to one knee to assist with the skirmish against the bikers still at the bar.

Shane tapped Julianna on the shoulder. "Come on inside. We'll leave out the back door and continue clearing the rest of the rooms."

She finished her magazine then followed Shane inside. Dan did likewise.

"Are we picking locks again?" Dan asked as they came to the back door of the next room.

"Yeah, but Bobby is using the big pick this time." Shane pointed to the shotgun on Bobby's back.

Bobby held the barrel of the shotgun out at an angle.

"Go!" Shane turned his head while Bobby blew out the lock, then he pulled the door open. Dan rushed in followed by Bobby, then Shane, then Julianna. They surprised three hostiles who'd been focused on the activity in the front of the motel. Shane's team was able to eliminate the bikers before they even knew they were present.

They continued down the row of motel rooms in like fashion. Inside each room, they encountered between two and four more hostiles, most of whom were totally inebriated and completely confused about what was going on. After successfully clearing seven rooms, Shane's team entered the next room with weapons drawn.

"Hold your fire!" Johnny stood inside the front door of the motel room with three other deputies at his side, all of whom had their weapons pointed at Shane and his team.

Shane lowered the barrel of his AR-15 and looked away. "You scared the devil out of me!"

Johnny suppressed a grin. "I guess you were coming in the back door while we were coming in the front."

Shane looked to make sure his team was okay. "All the rooms on that side are clear?"

"Yep," said Johnny. "Same for your side?"

"Everything between here and room 113 is clear." Shane looked out the back door. "Bunny started at the other end. If I can get his attention, we'll go help him finish up, but I don't want a repeat of what just happened."

"Okay, I'll take my team to help mop up at the bar. Sounds like the party is still going over there." Johnny took his men out the front door.

Shane led his team to room 113 by the back way. Once there, he passed through the motel room and peered out the front door. He saw Bunny and Wrench come out of a room three doors down.

Shane did his best to communicate via charades. He attempted to say to Bunny that he should take the room nearest to him, Shane's team would take the room next door and that they should meet in the middle. Bunny nodded that he understood, but Shane couldn't be sure that he had.

"Come on." Out the back once more, Shane took his team to the rear entrance of the adjacent room. Bobby blew off the lock with the shotgun and the team made entry. Four more stoned hostiles were eliminated and Shane led his troops to the front door.

"What are we waiting for?" Julianna stood behind him.

"I can't be sure Bunny understood what I was trying to tell him. I'm going to wait for them to enter the next room. That way, everyone should be aware of the people on the other team."

"Okay." She used the opportunity to switch magazines as did Dan and Bobby.

Shane listened. Boom! "That was the breach. Give them a few seconds to get inside, and we'll assist."

Shane waited a little longer. "Okay, let's wrap this up." He opened the front door and led his team to the next room. Once inside, he recognized the older woman who had the shotgun pointed at Bunny.

"Come on, now. You put that gun down, and I'll bring you back with me," Bunny said to the haggard woman with the 70s van mural on her back.

"You're a pig, ain't you? You sure played your part well." She held the gun low.

"I ain't no pig," said Bunny.

"Then what are you doing here? Who sent you?"

"I came on my own accord. Your club crossed the wrong folks. Most of 'em's dead." Bunny nodded and lowered his rifle. "But I'm your ticket out of here. You come on back with me. Start fresh."

Her eyes were bloodshot, her hair a mess, and she wore a terrycloth bathrobe which wasn't tied. This seemed not to bother her—at least not as much as it did Shane. The woman slowly shook her head. "Naw. I don't believe it. You're here with them pigs. You're a pig."

Shane knew she'd decided to shoot Bunny. He fired his rifle, striking her three times in the chest, but he was too late. She'd pulled the trigger and sprayed buckshot into Bunny's chest at close range. Wrench immediately dropped his rifle and went to his friend's side. However, he could do nothing. Bunny was gone.

Shane stood motionless, looking on at the biker who'd helped him so much.

"Come on." Julianna tugged at his arm. "You can't do anything for him. We need to get across the street. They're still shooting over there."

"Yeah." Shane looked up at his team. "Okay, let's go."

He changed magazines and hustled across the road. Johnny had three fire teams under his command. They were set up all the way around the bar.

"What's the situation?" Shane knelt low next to Johnny behind a big metal dragon sculpture in front of the bar.

"Best I can tell, we've about wiped them out. Might be ten or so of 'em holed up inside."

"What's the plan to get inside?"

"Rush 'em, I suppose."

Shane shook his head. "That will cost us. Someone will get killed."

"We have to finish this thing one way or the other. We can't very well leave them alive. They'll come back to Sylva for blood, even if that means hooking up with another gang." Johnny ducked low at the sound of small arms fire plinking off the opposite side of the dragon sculpture.

"We've got every angle of the building covered. If we could burn them out or smoke them out, we'd have no trouble picking them off." Shane made a careful observation of the bar.

Bobby looked at the still near the woods. "If that thing is full, we'll have no trouble getting accelerant."

Shane glanced back at the still. "Yeah, but we'd need containers to get it from there to here."

"Do you have a better idea?" Julianna asked.

Shane thought for a moment. "Maybe."

"Let's hear it," Johnny replied.

Shane looked at the old pick-up truck being used as a shield by some of the deputies. "If we light a piece of tire and get it inside, it would smoke them out."

"That thing will smoke like the dickens," said Dan. "But somebody will just pick it up and throw it right back out the door."

"They'll have to come to the door to pitch it out," Shane countered. "When they do, we'll pick them off."

"How long do you think you'll have to keep that up?" Julianna inquired. "Shooting one person at a time, then chucking the burning tire back inside."

"I'll do it as long as I have to," said Shane.

She lifted her shoulders. "If it were me, I'd just throw my jacket over it and put the fire out."

Shane grimaced at the lack of effort needed to bring his grand scheme to nothingness.

"They wouldn't be able to throw their jackets over it if the tire is outside," Dan added.

"What good would that do?" Shane inquired.

"The bar is covered in wood siding." Dan grinned. "The whole building will be like an Easy-Bake Oven in a matter of minutes. They'll come out, or they'll be roasted alive."

"Let's get those tires off." Shane crouched low and led his team to the old truck.

Once safely behind the vehicle, Dan opened the door and found the jack and tire tool. He passed the instruments to Bobby. "You work on removing the tires from this side of the truck. I'll see if I can get the spare from under the bed."

"I'll cover you," Julianna said to Dan. "If anyone

pokes their head out to take a shot at you, I'll blow it off."

Shane loosened the lug nuts of the front tire before Bobby jacked up the truck. Then, he moved to the rear tire while Bobby finished removing the wheel.

Dan pushed the spare out from under the bed of the truck, then emerged from beneath the vehicle.

"How are we going to get the tires to light?"

"Cut a strip out of the sidewall." Dan pulled out his knife and began cutting into the first tire. "We'll use that as a wick to get the blaze going."

Shane mimicked Dan's process and soon had a long slender strip of tire which should take a flame easily. "Now the fun part. We have to roll them to the building without getting shot."

Bobby completed the modifications on his tire. "We need lighters. Three of them."

Julianna looked at the deputies nearby. "Who has a lighter?"

Two of them tossed lighters to her.

"Anyone else?" she asked.

Shane began lighting his tire. "We should get them burning before we go." Once lit, he passed the lighter to Bobby. "I'll take my tire to the far side. Bobby, you go to the back and Dan will take his to the closest sidewall. I'll carry a lighter with me and so will Bobby. Dan, if your tire goes out, Bobby and I will both come by on our way back to cover. Either one of us can re-light your tire."

"Let's go for it." Dan got his tire burning, then handed off his lighter to Shane.

"Cover us!" Shane said to Julianna and the

deputies.

Johnny nodded from behind the big metal dragon that he was ready to cover Shane's team as well. Additionally, most of the Hill Riders had joined the fight at the bar and were in position to provide cover fire for the operation.

Shane took a deep breath, looked to heaven, and said, "God, watch over us, please!" He began rolling the flat, cumbersome, flaming wheel, being careful not to get any of the molten rubber on his hand and trying to avoid getting smoke in his eyes.

He heard Bobby's tire flop to the ground behind him. He turned back only for a second. "Come on. Get it back up. You can do it!"

Bobby managed to get the clumsy object upright once more and continued maneuvering it toward the building.

Gunshots rang out. Shane knew they'd originated from inside the bar. "Faster!"

Julianna and many others from the Sylva attack force peppered the bar with rifle fire in an attempt to subdue the assault from inside the building.

Once at his desired location, Shane leaned his tire against the wooden wall of the building. When the tire quit moving, the flame began to burn brighter and hotter.

He came from around the side to see Bobby propping his wheel against the rear wall. It also appeared to be burning well. The two of them sprinted to Dan's location. Likewise, his tire was in place and the blaze seemed to have survived the bumpy trip across the parking lot.

"Let's get back to cover and let the magic

happen." Shane prepared to lead the sprint to safety.

"Ready when you are," said Dan.

Bobby nodded.

"Go!" Shane darted out from the side of the building toward the truck.

Gunfire erupted from both sides.

"Ah!" Dan screamed.

Shane slid behind the cover of the pickup and looked back to see Dan lying on the ground. Blood was coming from his lower leg.

Bobby dropped to the ground and turned to go back for Dan. Shane rushed toward his fallen friend firing his rifle to cover Bobby who scooped Dan up from the ground.

Despite the heavy barrage of bullets fired by the Sylva group, the Iron Devils persisted in shooting from inside the bar.

"Get him out of here!" Shane continued shooting at the bar while Bobby hoisted Dan over his shoulder.

"Oh!" Bobby yelped.

Shane turned to follow the big man. He saw an ejection of blood spray from Bobby's bicep. Boom! Then another round struck Dan in the head.

Shane's stomach sank. Once they'd reached the safety of the pickup truck, he watched Bobby lower Dan to the ground. Shane put his finger to Dan's neck. "He's gone."

Bobby's gaze dropped low.

Shane pulled a tourniquet from the side pocket of his cargo pants. He wrapped it around Bobby's arm and tightened it. "Are you going to be okay?"

"Yeah." Bobby's voice sounded solemn. "Let's

get back in the fight."

Shane changed magazines and lay prone on the ground. He watched the flames begin to engulf the walls of the bar. Soon, the entire building combusted into a raging inferno.

A wave of Iron Devils stormed out of the bar with guns blazing. Shane and the rest of his group cut them down before they cleared the porch area. Others tried to flee the consuming torch but were also eliminated instantaneously. The escape attempts and gunfire from inside the bar slowed while the flames licked higher and higher. Once the blazing wood frame of the building became visible, the guns shots halted except for the occasional series of pops coming from exploding ammunition inside the bar.

Shane directed his attention to Bobby's bleeding arm. "Let's get you back to the truck and get a bandage on that."

"I'm going to carry Dan. We can't leave him here. He deserves better than that," Bobby tried to lift the dead body from the ground with his injured arm.

"Nobody is going to leave Dan. One of the others will bring him back." Shane attempted to restrain his friend.

"He came with us. It should be us who brings him back," Bobby argued.

"Then let me help you," said Shane.

"It would be easier if I carried him on my shoulder," countered Bobby.

"Then at least allow us to assist you in getting him up." Julianna placed her rifle on the ground.

Shane and Julianna tenderly lifted Dan's body and gingerly draped him over Bobby's big shoulder.

CHAPTER 10

All evils are to be considered with the good that is in them, and with what worse attends them.

Daniel Defoe, Robinson Crusoe

The drive back to Sylva was marked by sorrow. The team medic cleaned and bandaged Bobby's arm but urged him to go straight to the hospital where several volunteers were standing by to assist the single doctor and three nurses still keeping the facility open.

Shane kept his eyes on the road. "I'm going to hate this; telling his family. Kari will be another widow and Scott, another child who has to endure the cruel post-collapse world without a father. Every new dose of tragedy compounds the pain from the lives that have already been lost."

"We'll help them out." Julianna reached across the seat and took Shane's hand. "We'll make sure they have everything they need. It won't be easy, but Kari will survive. Scott will, too. They have to." She pulled her hand back. "I did when Will died. So did Cole. We didn't have a choice."

Minutes later, Julianna reached to take Shane's hand once more. "If he had it to do all over again, I don't believe Dan would change a thing. We eliminated the Iron Devils. Dan's wife and child are safe. What more could a father ask for?"

Shane drove with one hand, enjoying Julianna's touch on the other. "Safe for now. But like the flames of Gehenna, this fire is far from out. It's only a matter of time before the next threat emerges."

"I know." Julianna sighed. "But enjoy the victory for a little while. You've earned it."

The morning sun shone brightly by the time Shane returned to Sylva. The first stop was at the hospital. With his arm in a sling, Bobby opened the back door and stepped out.

"Do you think you'll be okay by yourself?" Shane turned around in his seat. "We need to tell Kari and Scott. Then we need to get Dan cleaned up so they can say goodbye. I'll come back as soon as we're done with that."

"Take your time. I'm sure they'll be bringing others back from Deal's Gap who need to be treated before me."

"Okay. But I'll come sit with you. I'll bring you something to eat also."

"I'll be here." Bobby waved with his available

hand.

Shane pulled away from the hospital. He drove slowly up the drive to James Teague's house where Angela, Cole, and Elizabeth Hayes were staying with Mrs. Betty. It was also where Kari and Scott Ensley waited for the safe return of Dan.

Shane put the vehicle in park and cut the ignition. Cole was the first to run out of the house. "Mama!" he shouted with glee at the sight of Julianna. "Shane!" he called to his father while still embracing Julianna.

Kari and Scott were next to appear. Kari looked around expectantly. "Where's Dan?"

Johnny Teague's wife and children came out onto the big porch. "Is Johnny okay?" his wife asked.

Shane answered Mrs. Teague first since her question had an easier answer. "Johnny is fine. He stayed behind to help wrap up."

Kari asked again. This time, her face showed concern. "Shane, where is Dan?"

Before he could reply, her face contorted into an expression of deep anguish, as if she already knew the grim response to her query.

Scott held her waist tightly, as if she might shield him from the mighty blow about to upend his fragile world. His worried eyes looked up at Kari. "Mama?"

Her lip quivered and she bent down to kiss him on the head. She knelt beside her son and pulled him to her bosom.

Shane squatted beside the two of them. "I'm so sorry. Dan was shot and killed at Deal's Gap. But I want you to know that his actions helped to secure our victory. Kari, you and Scott, as well as everyone else in Sylva are now safe from the Iron Devils because of Dan's sacrifice."

She listened as Shane spoke. She nodded with a forced smile which quickly gave way to a deluge of anguish. Mother and child wept bitterly.

Julianna sat on the porch next to her. She wrapped her arms around Kari and Scott. "We're here for you. I know it helps little right now, but you're not alone. And it sounds cliché, but I've been through what you're feeling right now. It may always hurt, but it will become bearable, with time."

Everyone else from inside the house came out. The news of Dan's death flowed from person to person via reverent whispers. Angela crossed her arms. Her face showed the sympathy she felt for Kari and Scott. "What about Bobby?"

"He was hit in the arm, but it's not life-threatening. I've got to go back to the hospital and get him after we get Dan cleaned up."

"I could go to the hospital to pick him up—if you need me to," Angela offered.

"The hospital is inundated with patients right now. There's no rush," said Shane. "Plus, I promised him I'd come back."

James Teague put his hand on Shane's shoulder. "You let me and Betty take care of preparing Dan. The wives will help us. You've been through enough. Go home, get yourself cleaned up. Get something to eat if you can. Rest and spend time with your boy."

Elizabeth Hayes volunteered, "I can stick around

to help out with Dan."

Shane felt his body getting more and more tired. "I appreciate that. Dan is in the bed of the truck."

After the Teagues had taken Dan's body from the bed of the truck. Shane, Angela, Cole, and Julianna returned to the Black compound.

"I'm going to get a quick shower at the guest cabin first," Shane said to Julianna as he pulled onto the property. "That way I can get back to the hospital."

"I wouldn't count on it," said Angela.

"Why is that?" Shane asked.

"Power has been out since you left."

"Great. I guess I'll be hauling buckets up from the spring." Shane pulled up to the house, killing the ignition to the truck.

"I can help bring water," Cole offered.

Shane smiled. "Thanks, buddy. I'll take you up on that."

***

An hour later, Shane packed the food Angela had prepared for Bobby into a paper sack. "I'll see you all later."

Julianna sat on the couch with Cole. "You should take a nap before you go. You've been up since yesterday morning. They wouldn't be able to see Bobby before noon on a normal day."

"I know. But if he has to sit and wait, I want to be there with him."

"Tell Bobby I said to get better soon." Angela waved.

"I will." Shane went to the Ram and headed toward the hospital. Just before arriving in town, Shane opened his eyes wide at the glaring horn of another vehicle. He'd drifted off to sleep at the wheel. The near-miss jolted him back to reality. He took a deep breath. "I must have swerved into that guy's lane." He rolled down the window and offered an apologetic wave. Shane looked closely at the other vehicle in the mirror. "A white Hummer!"

He made sure of what was in front of him, then checked the mirror once more. "Three more in front of that one!" Shane turned onto Asheville Highway to go to the hospital. He watched another convoy of UN vehicles drive down West Main Street. "I guess our time has come. I better see what I can do to get Bobby looked at quickly."

Shane parked the truck then sprinted across the parking lot to the hospital. Inside the waiting room, Shane spotted Bobby with his head back, fast asleep. He hated to wake his exhausted friend, but the message was urgent. "Hey, pal. Wake up."

Bobby sat up and looked around. He seemed unsure of his surroundings for a moment, then asked. "Did they call on me already? The woman at the desk said it might be tonight before they could get to me."

"I'm afraid that's not going to work." Shane relayed what he'd seen on the way to the hospital.

"I have to get this cleaned up." Bobby lifted his damaged arm in the sling.

"Yeah, I know. Wait here." Shane walked down the hall and found one of the volunteers. "Hey, do you know if Lisa Bivens is here?"

A young girl carried a box of clean linen strips that were likely being used for homemade bandages. "She is, but she's really busy. I think she's handling most of the sutures."

"I have an urgent message for her. Can you tell me where to find her?"

"The doctor is sending everyone that needs stitches to one of those rooms at the end of the hall."

"Thank you." Shane rushed back to the waiting room to collect Bobby. "Come on."

Bobby followed him down the hall.

Shane looked in the door of each of the rooms where deputies and members of the Hill Runners who'd been injured in the fight waited patiently for someone to care for their wounds.

Finally, Shane saw Lisa Bivens. He let himself in the room.

Lisa spun around. "Excuse me, you can't be in here right now."

"I'm sorry for barging in, but I have a favor to ask of you. I was good friends with your brother, Eric. My friend Bobby just has a bullet hole that needs to be cleaned out and stitched up."

The injured man she'd been sewing up said, "That's Shane Black."

"I know who he is, but that doesn't entitle him to preferential treatment. Besides, I'm a nurse practitioner. I can't diagnose what needs to be done for a bullet wound. He needs to see a doctor, and he needs to wait his turn."

The patient said, "The Iron Devils would be running this town right now if it weren't for Shane.

If he needs a doctor now, I'm sure he has a good reason. He can have my place in line. I'll go back to the waiting room."

Lisa looked at the wound she'd been stitching. After a long pause, she gave a sigh of exasperation. "I'll look at him. Bring him in here." She finished the patient she'd been working on while Shane brought Bobby into the room.

"What's going on? Why is this so urgent?"

Shane looked at the patient then Lisa. "This needs to stay in this room. I don't want to start a panic before we have all the details, but a UN convoy of at least ten vehicles just rolled down Main Street."

Lisa seemed to understand the direness of the situation. "I wish they were only here to help, but from the reports I've heard from around the country, the UN's help is coming at a very high price." She worked diligently to examine, clean, and stitch Bobby's wound. "It looks like it went straight through. You have a lot of tissue damage and in a perfect world, should have surgery." She looked up at Bobby. "But we're a good ways off from a perfect world at present."

"Thank you."

"Things should slow down in a day or two. Come back in, and let us have another look at that." She gave him a small vial of betadine. "Keep it as clean as possible. We're low on antibiotics, so we can't hand them out until we see confirmed signs of an infection."

"I appreciate it." Bobby put the sling around his neck and followed Shane out the door.

"We'll stop at the Teagues' first. Jimmy needs to know if he hasn't already found out." Shane raced out of the parking lot. He looked down Main Street on his way back to the Teagues but saw no sign of the armored vehicles.

Once back at the Teague compound, Bobby pointed at the vehicle in the drive. "Johnny is back."

"Good. He needs to know right away also." Shane sprung from the driver's seat and rushed to the front door where he knocked frantically.

James came to the door. "Shane, is everything okay?"

"Not really. Where is Johnny?"

"He's doin' what you ought to be doin'. Sleeping in the den." James replied.

"What about Jimmy?"

"I reckon he's at his office downtown. Why? What's all the fuss about?"'

Shane relayed what he'd seen on West Main Street.

"Come on in here. You best tell Johnny." James held the door for Shane and Bobby.

"Johnny." James shook the shoulder of his sleeping son. "Wake up, boy."

Johnny opened his eyes with a deep breath. He looked grumpy over having been disturbed. "What is it, Pop?"

"Shane is here. He's got something to tell you."

Johnny sat up on the couch. "What's going on?" He listened to Shane's description of what he'd seen.

"Jimmy is downtown. We better go see what's going on." Johnny stood up from the couch and put his feet into his boots.

"I'll drive." Shane led the way to the vehicle.

Ten minutes into the trip, Bobby pointed to an on-coming vehicle. "Is that Butterbean's patrol car?"

"Yep," said Shane. "He's flashing his lights. I better see what he wants." Shane slowed to a stop in the middle of the road.

Butterbean pulled up beside him and rolled down his window. "Shane!"

"What's going on?"

"Them soldiers took over the jail. Had some kinda letter. It looked official. Still, I wasn't gonna leave 'till the sheriff told me to, but they outnumbered us twenty to one. We didn't have no choice. They're lookin' for the sheriff. Want to talk to him."

Johnny rolled down the back window. "I'm here. We're headed downtown now."

"I don't believe you ought to go, Sheriff." Butterbean stuck his head further out the car window. "They took the mayor, kinda rough like."

"What do you mean, *took him*?" Shane put the truck in park.

"I mean, they came in asking him all kinds of questions. They wanted to know how he got to be mayor without no official election. They was askin' where was Mayor Hayes, even wanted to know about Sheriff Hammer."

"Who was doing the talking?" Johnny asked. "Was it one of the soldiers?"

"No. It was some woman in one of them business dresses."

"You mean like a skirt suit?" Shane inquired.

"I reckon," Butterbean replied. "Said she was some kinda Region Four Resource Administrator or somethin'. Rita Carmichael, I think."

"Is she American?" asked Shane.

"She was, but them soldiers weren't. Sounded Russian or somethin'. All of 'em was carrying AK-47s."

"Why don't you follow us to the Teague compound?" Shane put the truck in gear and began turning the wheel.

"That's where I was headed anyhow."

Shane sped back in the direction from which he'd just come. "We better keep you away from our visitors until we can ask them what's going on, Sheriff."

Johnny leaned forward in the back seat. "If you go over there, it might be best if you don't advertise that you're a deputy."

"We'll come up with some other pretense for our visit." Shane took the curves fast. "But we have to figure out what happened to Jimmy."

"I know Angela has no desire to see her husband." Johnny leaned over the front seat. "But Greg is still in the county lock-up. You could act as if you were taking her there for a visitation."

"Good idea. We'll drop you off and scoop her up, as long as she doesn't mind playing along." Shane drove even faster on the straightaways.

***

Half an hour later, Shane, Bobby, and Angela

walked up to the Jackson County Sheriff's Department. "This doesn't seem like a very good idea." Angela looked at the various white armored vehicles which filled the parking lot.

"Just play dumb. I don't think they're here to round up the townspeople." Shane walked slowly looking at the two peacekeepers guarding the front door.

"We are sorry, but department is closed temporarily," said one guard with a strong Eastern European accent.

"The sheriff's department is closed?" Shane acted confused. "Where is the sheriff?"

"We are in transitional phase. Should be everything sorted out by Monday. Are you here for report crime?"

"No, she's here to visit her husband. He's an inmate at the jail," said Shane. "Can we speak to the sheriff or whichever deputy is in charge?"

"UN is currently handling facility. Deputies were sent home and administrator is trying to figure out who is it should be the sheriff for this county. Seems there was some kind of—unofficial elections."

"Administrator? Who is the administrator?" Shane acted ignorant.

"Mrs. Carmichael. She is at mayor's office right now. She won't be available to see visitors until we have everything sorted out."

"At the mayor's office? Is she working with the mayor?" Shane pried for more information.

"Also is question about mayor," said the guard. "Because of unofficial election. Mrs. Carmichael is speak with him about this."

"Is the mayor in some kind of trouble?" Shane quizzed.

The guard shook his head. "No trouble. Just some questions."

"What about visitation?" Angela asked.

"No visitation this week, but could be that some inmate will be release if charge is non-violent. That's what we doing in most other city. We don't have means for care for people who got locked up for joint or steal can of soda. Maybe is going to come home soon, your husband." The guard smiled. "If he didn't kill somebody, that is."

"Thanks." Angela acted hopeful and grateful for the information.

"We appreciate your time." Shane waved at the guard.

"No problem."

Shane led the way back to the truck, taking inventory of the vehicles and making a mental note of everything else he saw. "I suppose we'll try to convince the Teagues to lay low. Give the situation some time to resolve itself. Maybe she'll cut Jimmy loose after she gets done speaking with him."

Bobby walked close to Angela. "Because that's what you would do if it were Julianna or one of us. Lay low, I mean. Wait for the situation to resolve itself."

"In a perfect world, yes. I'd wait—at least I'd try."

"Mmmhmm." Angela voiced her doubt.

***

Once home, Shane stopped by the guest cabin before returning to his trailer. Cole sat on the porch swing by himself. With one foot, he absentmindedly maintained a steady sway.

"Mind if I sit down?" Shane asked.

Cole seemed to emerge from his trance. "Sure." He slid over to make room for Shane.

"Where's Mama?"

"Sleeping." The young boy had none of his usual energy.

"Good. We had a long trip. She needs her rest."

Cole didn't answer. He was quiet for several minutes. Finally, he asked, "Is Mama going to die?"

"What?" Shane shook his head. "No."

"How can you be so sure? Daddy died—I mean, Will."

"That's okay, you can call him Daddy. It doesn't hurt my feelings. Will earned that title from you. He loved you very much. And I love you very much also."

Cole continued. "Grandma and Grandpa Black died. Pastor Joel died. Now Scotty's dad is dead. Are you going to die?"

Shane searched his heart for a good answer, one that wasn't a dismissive placation. "I know. I miss them all. The truth is, we're all going to die someday. But, if you love Jesus, trust in Him and His sacrifice, we'll all be together again on the other side. Once we get there, we won't have any more sorrow or dying."

Cole appeared unconsoled. "I know about all of that. But I need Mama now." His eyes welled up.

Shane pulled him close. "I know. And I think God knows that. It's why I believe He's going to look out for Mama, take care of her and always bring her back to you."

The boy wiped his eyes. "You really believe that?"

"I do."

After several minutes of allowing Shane to console him, Cole perked up. He got out of the swing. "Thanks, Shane. I'm going to walk down to the creek."

"Do you want me to come with you?"

"You had a long trip, too. You should probably get some rest also."

Shane smiled at the boy who was wise beyond his years. "Okay. I'll see you in the morning."

CHAPTER 11

When anyone hears the word of the kingdom, and does not understand it, then the wicked one comes and snatches away what was sown in his heart. This is he who received seed by the wayside. But he who received the seed on stony places, this is he who hears the word and immediately receives it with joy; yet he has no root in himself, but endures only for a while. For when tribulation or persecution arises because of the word, immediately he stumbles. Now he who received seed among the thorns is he who hears the word, and the cares of this world and the deceitfulness of riches choke the word, and he becomes unfruitful. But he who received seed on the good ground is he who hears the word and understands it, who indeed bears fruit and produces: some a hundredfold, some sixty, some thirty."

Matthew 13:19-23 NKJV

Shane leaned his guitar against the trunk of the chestnut tree after worship Sunday morning. While Julianna made her way to her seat under the shade of the massive chestnut, he noticed that Kari and Scott still had not made it to the service. He also observed the grim expressions on the faces of the Teague family, particularly those of Jimmy's wife and children. He bowed his head and offered a prayer. He asked for God to bring Jimmy home soon and to comfort the Ensleys in their time of grief.

Taking a deep breath, he opened Pastor Joel's Bible and read the parable of the sower. Afterward, he looked up at his dwindling, beleaguered congregation. "Three times, the Bible says that man shall not live by bread alone, but by every word that proceedeth out of the mouth of God. This statement first appears in Deuteronomy then it is quoted by Jesus when He is being tempted by Satan. Two accounts of that incident show up. Once in Matthew 4:4 and again in Luke 4:4.

"My point being, that given the limited amount of real estate in the 66 books of the Bible, if God saw fit to include this single line three times, it must be important. Think about what God is saying. His words sustain our spirits in the same way that bread keeps our bodies going. Since the collapse, we've all wondered what it would be like to starve to death. By the grace of God, we've fared better than most of the country, but we all recognize that it could happen. We've heard the stories from around the country. People are at the end of their ropes.

"While we've had sufficient food so far, we've also had our fair share of trouble. I have to admit, I've allowed worry to get in the way of reading the Bible. It's easy to make an excuse out of it. After all, we only have so much time in the day. Since the collapse, even when we're not in a firefight, it seems we have more chores to do than ever. It seems we always have something more urgent that needs attending to than reading the Bible. I think that's valid. Perhaps all these things are more urgent. But that doesn't make them more important."

He held up the Bible. "If this book contains the very words of life, what could possibly be more important? Bread? Something that keeps this body going for another day?"

Shane shook his head. "This body is going in the dirt sooner or later, regardless of what I do to maintain it. My spirit, however, that's eternal. So what is more important than reading this book? Air? Water? Nothing. Man doesn't live by bread alone. It's every word from the mouth of God, that's what sustains us.

"So what does all of this have to do with the parable of the sower? My explanation contains a confession, so please bear with me.

"I lost this concept somewhere along the way.

When I was younger, I made time for God's Word every day. Then, as I began pursuing my music career, my devotion time got pushed to the back burner. The next thing you know, it wasn't even on the stovetop. One thing led to another, and I became the third type of soil Jesus mentioned in the parable. My life was inundated with thorns. The cares of this world and the deceitfulness of wealth choked out the life-giving words of God. My life became fruitless. Worse than that. I let down the people I loved. I failed to honor my father and mother. I abandoned Julianna. I cast my life upon the altar of Shane Black. However, I didn't make a very good god. Despite my absolute devotion to self, I failed at making myself happy. I won't lie to you and tell you I didn't enjoy any of it. But it was hollow. Those good times had no substance and they didn't satisfy me.

"I've repented of that to God. I've apologized to Julianna—and Cole. I even had the chance to reconcile with Mom and Dad before they died. But what I'm trying to say, is that it doesn't have to be fortune and fame that causes you to lose focus, to become dissipated and unfocused. It can be something as basic as trying to survive from one day to the next.

"A thousand years from now, when we're all at home with Jesus, none of it will matter. The Country Music Awards I've won and the battles I've fought against the Iron Devils will all be in the same dust bin. But the time invested in feeding my spirit, the minutes spent consuming the Bread of Life, that's what will count.

"I know you're busy. I'm not asking you to neglect your daily needs or responsibilities. I don't believe that's biblical either. But make time for God. Make time for His Word. Make it a priority. And if you plan on giving Him time at the end of the day when everything else is done, you're planning to give Him nothing. Because that's always what's leftover." Shane bowed his head to pray, then dismissed the congregation.

Lunch consisted mostly of fresh vegetables from the gardens. Tomatoes, squash, green beans, butterbeans, and a big plate of cornbread. Shane meandered through the line, still not fully rested from the action in Deal's Gap. Julianna and Cole got in line behind Shane. She said, "That was a good message. Your parents would have been proud."

"Thank you." The three of them sat at one of the big picnic tables after filling their plates.

Johnny and his father, James, sat at the same table. "That was some fine preachin'," said James. "Most of 'em that gets up there acts like they ain't never done no wrong. Takes a big man to point out his own shortcomin's. Heaven knows plenty of other folk don't mind doin' it for you."

"I appreciate that." Shane continued eating.

"We're taking your advice about seeing if the issue with Jimmy will resolve itself," said Johnny. "But if we haven't heard from him by tomorrow morning, we have to do something."

"What do you have in mind? They're armed to the teeth, outnumber us two to one, and have armored vehicles," said Shane.

"I don't know. At the very least we need to go talk to them. If talking doesn't work, we'll have to see about getting the Hill Runners involved," Johnny stared at the food on his plate.

"Sounds suicidal." Shane took a bite of green beans.

"What would you have us do?" James lowered his brow. "If it was your boy in there, ain't nothin' in the world you wouldn't do to get him out."

"No. I guess there isn't. Whatever you decide, I'll support you. But we need to get the women and children out to Dan's place in Murphy—I suppose it's Kari's place now. We'll have to ask her if she's okay with that." Shane let his fork rest on the side of his plate.

"You might not have to wait until tomorrow." Shane stood up from the table to see a line of white armored vehicles barreling up his gravel drive. "Julianna, get Cole and take him inside. If you see trouble, go out the back and cut through the woods to the Franzes'."

"I'm going to fight. Angela can watch Cole." She got up from her seat.

"I need you to do this. Please! We don't stand a chance against a force this big."

"Then run with us." She picked Cole up.

"I can't. It's my property. I have to see what they want."

"Shane!" Her eyes implored him to come.

"Just go! Go now while you still can!" Shane gave her a gentle nudge.

Johnny and James ushered the other women and children to leave the immediate area.

Three white Humvees turned off the gravel road and drove down by the creek. Other UN vehicles raced up the drive, cutting in behind Shane's group. Shane reached for his pistol but then decided against drawing it. Bobby looked at Shane for direction. "They've got us. If we fight, we're dead for sure."

Johnny nodded to some of the other men around. "Shane's right. Let's try to resolve this peaceably."

Shane looked to see Julianna, Angela, and Cole fleeing up the hill into the woods with Carrol Franz and Elizabeth Hayes. He brought his attention back to the UN troops pouring out of their vehicles with rifles drawn. The door of the vehicle closest to him opened. Out stepped an older man who appeared to be in command. The passenger's side door opened and a familiar face came into view. It was Greg Harper, Angela's sell-out of a husband.

"That's Shane," Greg pointed to his estranged brother-in-law. He then turned his index finger toward the sheriff. "And that's Johnny Teague."

"What's this about?" Shane asked.

The older man removed his blue helmet and held it under his arm. His English was very good, but his Eastern European accent was still thick. "I'm Commander Abdulov. The Regional Administrator, Rita Carmichael, requests to speak with the two of you, Mr. Black and Mr. Teague. Will the two of you please come with me?"

"Is that a request or a command?" Shane asked.

Abdulov smiled. "Consider it a firm request."

"Can I decline the invitation?" Shane asked.

Abdulov shook his head and spoke to his troops

in his own language.

Four of them went to Shane. They cuffed him and took his pistol. Four others did the same to Johnny.

"You devils don't know what you're starting here!" James Teague shook his finger at the men in blue helmets.

Shane shook his head at Bobby, signaling for him to stand down. He went peaceably as they escorted him to the back of one of the transport vehicles. Johnny was seated next to Shane. The doors closed and the convoy left as quickly as it had arrived.

Shane looked out the window at the familiar scenery on the way downtown. Everything else about the trip was completely out of place. "Scooping us up on a Sunday. I guess she wants to talk pretty bad."

"No telling what lies that sniveling Greg Harper has told her," Johnny scowled.

Shane couldn't get comfortable with his hands cuffed behind his back. "Was that just my imagination or did it look like Greg had been assigned some kind of role with the UN?"

"He didn't have on a uniform, but he wasn't wearing jail clothes either." Johnny fidgeted.

When they arrived at the municipal hall, the doors to the transport vehicle opened. Shane and Johnny were pulled out with no pretenses of courtesy.

Shane recognized yet another familiar face, Gary Hicks, the former Sylva PD officer commonly referred to as Lurch. Hicks rifled through Johnny's pockets.

"What do you think you're doing?" Johnny protested but could do nothing as his escorts held him by the arms.

Hicks retrieved Johnny's wallet, removed the sheriff's badge, and then stuck the wallet back in his pocket. "I've been assigned interim constable."

"By who?" Johnny demanded.

"By the mayor." Hicks pinned the star upon his own chest.

Wallace Hayes stepped out of the building. "Shane. So good to see you again. I wish it were under better circumstances, but you've brought all of this on yourself."

Shane glared at the man who'd been a harbinger of trouble every time the two had crossed paths.

Hayes chuckled at Shane's misery. "I see you've been reacquainted with Jackson County's Deputy Constable as well." Hayes held out his hand toward Greg who was getting out of the lead vehicle with Commander Abdulov.

"Tell me I'm dreaming," Johnny whispered to Shane.

"If you are, I'm stuck in the same nightmare." Shane struggled to keep his balance as he was roughly pushed toward the door.

Once inside, Wallace Hayes knocked on the door of his old office. "Mrs. Carmichael, the people you wanted to speak with have arrived."

"Thank you, Wallace. You can send them in."

Hayes opened the door like a poorly-paid errand boy. Behind his old desk sat a gaunt woman with hair dyed an unnatural red. The woman looked to be in her late fifties and seemed rather uptight. "Mr. Black, Mr. Teague, how good of you to join us."

She waved her hand at the guards. "You may leave us. I can't imagine they can cause too much trouble with their hands cuffed behind their backs. I'll call you if I need you."

The guards left but Hayes remained in the office.

"Wallace, you, too. Out." She waved her hand like someone might shoo away an unwanted pet.

Hayes closed the door behind himself.

"Please, take a seat." Carmichael motioned toward the chairs in front of her desk.

Shane and Johnny sat down.

Carmichael looked through some handwritten notes on a yellow legal pad. "I've been hearing some stories about the two of you."

"Every story has two sides," said Shane.

"I realize that. It's why I've brought you in." She crossed her hands and let them rest on top of the legal pad. "Let's start with the mayor's accusations about his abduction."

"It goes back farther than that ma'am. We'd have to begin with a brief history of the political corruption in Jackson County, which originates with Wallace Hayes' political action committee and his construction company."

"I haven't got time for all of that. I've spoken with Jimmy Teague, your brother, I believe." She looked at Johnny then continued. "I've heard his allegations of corruption. I suppose there must have been some merit to it in order for the entire town to come out in a referendum election. But even so, it doesn't justify kidnapping and some of the other things I've heard."

"Then why has Hayes been reinstated?" Johnny asked.

"Because all elections have been suspended until the crisis abates. Federal, state, and local. In cases where a vacancy arises, interim officers are to be appointed by the official immediately above the position. I'm sure you've noticed, our country is operating in survival mode. We need to work together if we're going to have anything other than a heap of ashes once the smoke clears."

"Hayes told you he was abducted, but did he tell you he set up a kangaroo court to convict and hang those accused of being involved? We're talking a couple of days from arrest to execution. No jury, no right to appeal, absolute disregard for due process," Johnny said.

Carmichael jotted down some notes on her legal pad. "I've heard the accusations. And while the way Mayor Hayes handled things is disturbing, you should know that the Constitution has been temporarily suspended. The country is facing a systemic failure, and we don't have the resources to allocate to the 200-year-old notion of how people thought the world should be."

"Plenty of us still think it should be that way," said Shane.

Carmichael replied, "I'm sure you do, but that experiment has failed. It has failed miserably and utterly. It's time we tried something new."

"New? Like what? Totalitarian socialism?" Shane asked. "Nothing new about that. You want to talk about an experiment that has failed over and over. The only thing socialism has going for it is a consistent track record of complete catastrophe. The Constitution isn't what caused this mess, it's our country's inability to adhere to the principles therein."

"So, you'll admit, it was unable to stop the collapse. The document could not stand up under the burden of capitalism."

Shane's eyebrows drew together. "Capitalism? We haven't had capitalism in this country since FDR. Capitalism isn't what's on trial here anyway. We had a currency collapse. Fiat currency is the culprit. When you allow a government to print money until it becomes absolutely worthless, that's exactly what they'll do, every time. That's another one which is batting a thousand."

"You seem very sure of your perceptions." Carmichael offered a thin smile.

"Aren't you sure of yours?"

"I suppose I am." She waved her hand at the ceiling. "And I'm sure we could go on and on about this late into the evening, and I doubt very much either one of us would persuade the other. It matters little anyhow, what you or I think. We're not the ones in charge."

"Although you seem to be more so than us," Shane countered.

Rita Carmichael appeared pleased by that statement. "Now we've found something we both agree on, common ground. I think that's important if we're going to move forward. We can agree to disagree as long as we can remain civil and do it with mutual respect."

"What does moving forward mean?" Johnny asked.

"It means my office will be able to pursue our goals with your cooperation."

"May I ask what, exactly, your office is, and what your goals are?" Shane inquired.

"I believe that's a fair question." She nodded. "My title is ESC Region 4, Sector D-6 Resource Administrator. My office's goals are to direct the flow of resources in and out of Region 4, Sector D-6. For all of its wordiness, it actually means what it says, rather utilitarian and direct, wouldn't you say?"

Shane considered the title and the implications. "How did you come to be employed by the ESC and the UN?"

"I worked in logistics with FEMA for more than two decades. This is right up my alley. Most FEMA personnel were absorbed by the Economic Stability Commission."

"When you say the flow of resources in and out of Region 4, Sector..." Johnny seemed unable to remember the entire string.

"D-6," Carmichael said. "Sector D-6 consists of Jackson, Swain, and Graham Counties."

"D-6," Johnny continued. "What resources are you talking about?"

"This part of the country has a lot of forests. We'll be logging much of that for export. We'll also be examining ways to exploit the agricultural potential."

"You might have noticed on your way in," Johnny smirked. "But half the land around here angles up at a fairly steep incline. The other half slopes down just as sharply. We're doing good if we can find a spot to plant a quarter-acre garden. This ain't the best land for mass agricultural production."

"Maybe not for corn or soybeans, but apple trees and the like aren't as picky about hills." She folded her hands on the yellow pad of paper once more. "Even so, the timber alone is quite valuable."

"So, you're planning to clear cut all the forest lands around here?" Shane asked. "Doesn't that go against the whole climate change agenda that the UN is so dogmatic about?"

"It doesn't have to be a contradiction of the UN's policy on preserving the planet. Pines and bamboo can be planted to replace the hardwood forests. They'll quickly replace the harvested trees in eliminating CO_2."

Shane's stomach soured at the thought of the beautiful landscape being destroyed. Never in a million years did he think he'd be the tree-hugger when it was between himself and a UN employee. "You also mentioned resources flowing in."

"That's right," said Carmichael. "We'll be reconnecting basic phone service, turning the lights back on, making sure the area has adequate medical services. We'll supplement nutritional needs until the region has the ability to reengage with the global marketplace."

"Why us?" Johnny asked. "Why bring all these troops, vehicles, and equipment out to the middle of nowhere?"

"The short answer is that the cities are falling apart. We have a limited amount of time, manpower, and energy that can be allocated to this effort, so we'd rather focus on places that can be saved. If you have one doctor, and ten patients, it might not be the best use of the physician's time to treat the four people who are terminally ill.

"But as I mentioned before. I believe we can extract a decent amount of value from the region."

"Why did you bring us in? Are we under arrest?" Shane inquired.

"I'm still considering what to do with you, but I'm inclined to give you another chance." She stared at the two of them for a while. "If I let you go, will you consent to my office's authority?"

"We don't really have a choice," said Johnny.

"That's not the answer I'm looking for," she replied.

"We'll consent." Shane lowered his gaze.

"That's better." Rita Carmichael gave another of her insincere smiles. "That will include the mayor and anyone he appoints to assist him in the task of local governance."

"I respect your position ma'am, but Wallace Hayes has a history of abusing power," Shane said.

"Let me worry about Hayes. I'll be providing oversight. You can bring any perceived abuse to my attention and I'll address it."

"Yes, ma'am." Shane didn't like any of it, but he was in no position to argue.

"Guard," she called.

Four men with blue helmets rushed into the room.

Carmichael pointed to Shane and Johnny. "Remove the cuffs from Mr. Black and Mr. Teague.

You can also bring the other Teague over from the jail. He is to be set free as well."

Shane rubbed his wrists. "They took our weapons when we were brought in. May we please get those back?"

"Firearms are banned for civilians." She looked down at her note pad.

"Banned? Since when?" Johnny asked.

"Since the ESC took control." Her eyebrows lifted.

"But the criminals still have guns. How are we supposed to defend ourselves?" asked Shane.

"We'll handle security concerns." She added, "Additionally, my men removed the rifles, pistols, and ammunition found at your two compounds. Is that going to be a problem?"

Shane knew he'd been beaten. "I guess not."

The guard asked, "When other Teague is coming here, do you want I give it ride home for them?"

She paused as if considering how to answer or perhaps deciphering the broken English of the guard. Finally, Carmichael said, "No. They can walk. They seem a little upset over the situation. It will be a good opportunity for them to let off some steam."

CHAPTER 12

Of all tyrannies, a tyranny sincerely exercised for the good of its victims may be the most oppressive.

C.S. Lewis

Shane, Jimmy, and Johnny walked the long winding road home. "Feels like a hundred degrees out here!" Shane squeegeed the sweat from his forehead with his fingers and wiped his hand on his shirt.

"It's the humidity. I doubt the temperature is over eighty-five." Johnny drew deep breaths as the three men marched up an inclining curve.

"The least they could have done is give us a bottle of water for the trip," said Jimmy.

Shane maintained an even stride. "This is

supposed to be a lesson in who's boss."

"Yeah?" Johnny turned to his brother. "And how do we feel about that?"

"They've got the guns and the men to pull the triggers," Jimmy replied. "I guess they're the boss."

"All the guns?" Shane asked.

"Pop and I buried a bunch of the AK-47s we took from the Iron Devils." Johnny paused to catch his breath. "We took a page from your playbook."

"Yeah, I wish I had been more proactive. I never got a chance to stash any weapons." Shane waited for Johnny to continue walking. "We hadn't even been back for a full twenty-four hours when Commander Abdulov showed up. I do still have some of the gold which Dad and I put in the ground. If you two decide we should fight, I'll dedicate what I can to the war effort."

"If *we* decide?" Johnny continued up the hill. "You'll have as much say in it as anyone else."

Shane focused on the pavement under his boots. "More fighting means more death. I don't see any point in getting a bunch of people killed just to lodge our grievance."

"I agree," said Jimmy. "If we don't stand a chance at winning, I have no interest in starting a war."

The tenuous ten-mile trek, which took them up and down tall hills and short mountains, finally came to an end. Shane waved at the weary brothers when they turned off to the Teague compound, then continued up the road another half mile to his own.

"Shane!" Bobby was the first to see him. He came running up to his old friend. "You look rough.

Did they hurt you?"

"No. Just made us walk home. But I suppose that was cruelty enough in this heat." Shane plopped down in the shade just inside the metal gate. "I could use a drink of water."

"I'll get my canteen. Wait here." Bobby sprinted away in the direction of the trailers.

Shane removed his boots and moved his toes. He enjoyed the cool feeling of having only his sweaty socks on his feet.

Bobby returned in a matter of minutes. He handed the large canteen to Shane. "They let Johnny go also?"

"Yep." Shane chugged a long drink then wiped his mouth. "Jimmy, too. Did Julianna come back?"

"No. They stayed at the Franzes'. Kari and Scott are still here. I thought Scott was going to kill one of those UN soldiers when they took Dan's guns. He didn't like that at all."

"No. I suppose not." Shane tipped up the bottom of the canteen once more. "Did they get all the guns?"

Bobby pulled up his shirttail to reveal the handle of a pistol. "I had this one tucked up beneath the axle of my trailer. But I've only got one box of ammo for it. The guards seemed convinced that they should have found guns in the guest cabin but didn't. They carted some ammo out of there though."

Shane smiled. "Julianna and Angela, they took their rifles to the Franzes'." His elation faded. "Even so, it won't make a hill of beans up against the heavily armed peacekeepers."

"You may be right about that, but at least we're not completely defenseless."

"The Teagues have a few AKs stashed—from Deal's Gap. However, I don't think they have much ammo."

"What did the UN have to say? Did you talk to the administrator?"

"Rita Carmichael, yeah, we had a nice long chat." Shane debriefed Bobby on the conversation.

"Hmm. That's interesting, especially in the context of what's going on with the rest of the world."

"Oh yeah?" Shane waited for Bobby to continue.

"Yep. I didn't want to bother Kari and Scott. They seem like they want to be left alone to grieve. Didn't have much else to do but listen to NPR. All international currencies are expected to tank when the markets open tomorrow. The IMF is planning to roll out the block-chain edition of the SDR, hoping it will be accepted by global markets as the new global currency. If not, the reporter said tomorrow will be the end of the world economic system. Markets are expected to suffer a catastrophic meltdown."

Shane remained on the side of the gravel road. "That would be frightening news if we weren't already living in a nightmare." He pulled his socks off and tucked them halfway into his boots. "Are the central banks of the world on board with this call?"

"Most of them. Everyone except China, Russia, and OPEC. They're each moving to gold."

"What? They're going to take gold coins at the

grocery store in those countries?"

"China is supposedly coming out with a gold-backed currency."

"They don't own that much gold, something like 2,000 tonnes, I think."

"Evidently, the official count was off. They're reporting that they now have 30,000 tonnes."

Shane shook his head. "Impossible. Someone would have noticed them accumulating that much. They couldn't have sourced it all domestically."

"NPR is speculating that the PBOC had proxy buyers set up. They think China has been quietly preparing for a new monetary regime over the past two decades. Besides that, unlike here, China encourages its citizens to own gold."

Shane rubbed his head. "I suppose it's to be expected in an age where central bankers don't allow audits. If they did, it would have been discovered long ago that the US had far less than the reported 8,000 tonnes."

"What about OPEC? None of those countries have enough gold to back a currency." Shane finished off the water in the canteen.

"Maybe not, but by selling oil in gold, they will eventually."

Shane said, "If the SDR solution doesn't work, the IMF is toast. So is the UN, the ESC, and so is Rita Carmichael."

"Sounds like you're wishing for it to fail."

Shane shook his head. "I'm not so sure about that. Right now, we're under the control of a bunch of self-appointed, self-righteous, autocrats who think they know what's best for everyone else. But they're the last vestige of civility. If they perish, the power vacuum left behind will be filled by someone far worse, someone who doesn't concern themselves with the pretenses of being humane. It's been a long ride down from where we were, but I'm not ready to call this the bottom."

"The sun will be setting soon. Should I go tell Julianna and the others that you're home?"

Shane nodded. "Yes. We'll need to hide some of those weapons when they get back. The peacekeepers could come back at any time to do another inspection. I'd come with you, but I've had my share of traveling for the day. If you don't mind, I'm going to get cleaned up and find something to eat."

"Go right ahead. I'll see you when I get back."

***

August 1st, nine days after Shane's meeting with Rita Carmichael.

Shane ran to the door of his trailer to see who was pounding on it so early in the morning. "Julianna, is everything okay?"

Her eyes were bright and happy. "Yes, everything is great! We've got electricity!"

"That's awesome!" Shane looked around to think of what he should do first.

"Do you have any clothes you want to be washed?"

"All of them, probably. I've been keeping up with laundry, but hand-washed in a bucket doesn't feel as clean as a freshly-washed load out of the dryer."

"How about you give me a load now. If the power is still on this evening, we'll do another load for you. We've got eight people sharing one washing machine, so it's going to take some time just to do one pile for each of us."

"Oh, right," said Shane. "I'll get everything together and bring it over to the house in a bit. I'll work on making sure all the batteries are charged. That single solar charger takes forever."

"Great." She looked him over. "You might want to bring a change for a hot shower. I'd forgotten how wonderful one of those feels."

"Good suggestion. I'll take you up on that." He watched her walk away.

Shane quickly gathered a load of clothes. Next, he collected batteries from flashlights and walkie-talkies, then took them to the house to charge. He headed to Bobby's trailer afterward and told him the good news.

Bobby grabbed the AM/FM radio and brought it with him as he followed Shane back to the house. The two of them met Elizabeth Hayes and Kari Ensley coming from the house with a collection of baskets and containers.

"Where are you ladies going?" Shane asked.

"To pick vegetables. It's a whole lot easier to do canning on an electric stove than over the coals of an open fire," said Elizabeth.

"It's a lot easier to clean up the mess with running water, too," Kari added.

"I'll send Cole down to help when I see him,"

said Shane.

"He's with Scott. They're finishing breakfast, and they'll both be along in a while," Kari replied.

"I'll come help also," Shane waved as they walked by.

Bobby added, "Me, too." Once out of earshot, Bobby commented, "Kari seems to be doing better. Scott also."

"It's a hard thing to deal with. I'm sure they'll always miss Dan, but the apocalypse keeps you busy. None of us have time to sit around and sink into depression."

Once Shane had loaded rechargeable batteries into every charger he could locate, he and Bobby joined the others at the garden. Bobby and Shane worked side-by-side in the field so they could both listen to the radio.

The male NPR reporter had a soft voice. "The new digital SDR has stopped falling in value against gold and other commodities for the last two trading sessions. Since the implementation of the new digital global currency last Monday, the SDR has lost two-thirds of its value when denominated in gold.

"Economists see this as a positive sign, which may indicate the new currency is gaining acceptance. The digital SDR has been put into full effect across Europe and is serving as the only unit of exchange across the EU. Canada and Australia have also made much progress in completing the transition with more than 80 percent of retailers now using the SDR exclusively. South American countries are a mixed bag, with some near 70 percent implementation and others struggling to achieve 50 percent.

"Surprisingly, the country having the lowest success is the one who needs it the most. Estimates put the US at below 10 percent of the country using the new currency, but that is thought to be due to the failed state of so many larger US metropolitan areas. ECS commissaries are now accepting digital SDRs anywhere in America where relief centers are capable of operating without the threat of looting and violence."

Elizabeth spoke up from two rows over. "Mandy Teague says they have one of those commissaries set up across the street from the old paper mill. Supposedly, they have shampoo, deodorant, soap, rice, beans, all kinds of stuff."

"Who has SDRs to buy anything from them?" Bobby asked.

Shane pitched a handful of green beans into his bucket. "The UN soldiers do, I'm sure."

"The paper mill workers, too," said Elizabeth Hayes. "Mandy says the ESC Resource Department has had it up and running for a week now."

"Shane!" Cole ran over carrying an arm full of tomatoes. "Those people are back!"

Shane looked up to see a white Jeep with a light-blue UN painted on the hood coming up the drive. He took the tomatoes from his son and placed them in the bucket on top of the green beans. He patted Bobby on the shoulder. "Are you packing?"

Bobby pulled the pistol from his waistband and

handed it to Shane. Shane hid the weapon under the green beans. And handed the bucket to Cole. "Take this up to the house. Give it to Mama. Tell her the people are back and tell her to hide what's in the bucket."

Cole nodded that he understood and skedaddled up the hill to the house.

Shane looked over to Kari, Scott, and Elizabeth. "Y'all stay in the garden and keep your heads down. Bobby and I will go see what they want."

He led the way up to the gravel drive. The Jeep rolled to a stop. Two armed peacekeepers exited the vehicle before a woman stepped out. She had blonde hair pulled back into a ponytail, wore a white polo shirt with the UN insignia and carried a clipboard.

"Why does she look familiar?" Shane couldn't quite place her.

Bobby answered. "That's Tessa. Scofield's girl."

Shane noticed the tattoos beginning at her wrists and disappearing under her shirt sleeves. "Oh, right. This certainly is a different look for her."

He waited for them to get closer then asked, "How can I help you?"

Tessa tore a sheet of paper off of her clipboard to give to Shane. "Work orders, for your group."

Shane looked at the paper. "Work orders?"

"Yeah, seems the shoe is on the other foot now, Mr. Black. But don't you worry. I'm not holding it against you for killing all of my friends and leaving me in that horrible jail to rot."

Shane read the text on the document received from Tessa. "Three days a week working with a timber harvesting crew."

"Yes." Her smile beamed. "That's for every member of your compound between the ages of 16 and 65. You'll need to fill out the days each of you is available to work. If you require transport, the ESC Resource Department will pick you up at the bottom of your driveway, but you'll need to be there an hour before your scheduled work time."

"This is insane!" Shane shook the paper at her. "There's no way we're going to participate in this forced slave labor program."

"I was hoping you'd say that." She grinned. "If you refuse, you'll be taken to a residential work camp. If you refuse to work there, you'll be placed in solitary confinement where you'll be fed bread and water. Do you have children, Mr. Black?"

Shane kept his jaw tight. He wasn't about to disclose anything that would endanger Cole, nor provide further vulnerabilities for himself.

Tessa added, "We have camps for them as well."

"Who decides which jobs are assigned and by whose authority is this program being put into place?"

"The ESC instituted the program. They decide how many people are needed to complete various tasks. Then, they hand it off to the local administrators to assign individuals. I met a guy coming out of jail who recommended me to the mayor. He gave me a job in HR for the ESC's work program. So, I'm the one who says who does what. This is the worst job available—for now. But as soon as we can get sanitation services back up and running, I'll make sure you get reassigned."

Shane looked back down at the paper. "10 SDRs per day. What does that amount to? Like $15 dollars in pre-crash terms?"

"Your mandatory service also provides for electricity, property taxes, water, and weekly food rations."

Shane wadded up the paper and tossed it on the ground. "We have our own water, we grow our own food, and you can cut our electricity back off if it means being forced into slavery. Besides all of that, my taxes are paid up through the next two decades."

"Can you provide documentation of that? And might I ask if those advance taxes were paid to a legitimate treasury office? I'll remind you, any agreement you may have had between you and your little buddies doesn't stand. Anyway, it's not up to you. The work program is mandatory. No exceptions." She pointed to the wrinkled paper on the ground. "I'd pick that up and dust it off if I were you. Have it filled out and returned to the personnel resource office by lunch tomorrow." She opened the door of the Jeep and got inside. "It's in the municipal building downtown."

Shane picked up the paper and smoothed it out. "Dan Ensley's name is on here. He's dead."

"Let me guess. He was killed by outlaws in Deal's Gap. Forgive me if I don't look grief-stricken. I'm absolutely bawling on the inside." She rolled up her window and the Jeep drove away.

"What are you thinking?" Bobby asked.

Shane stared at the form. "I'm thinking we don't have any other choice. We'll have to split up the workdays so that someone is always here for the kids. You and I will also have to take opposite days so there's always a man around for added security."

"Julianna isn't going to like this." Bobby shook his head.

Shane frowned. "Nobody is going to like this."

CHAPTER 13

If socialists understood economics they wouldn't be socialists.

Friedrich Hayek

Shane, Julianna, and Elizabeth Hayes waited at the bottom of the drive on Monday morning, not knowing what to expect out of their new job assignments. Shane's group would work Mondays, Wednesdays, and Fridays while Bobby, Kari, and Angela would take Tuesdays, Thursdays, and Saturdays.

"At least if we drove, we could avoid standing out here for who knows how long every morning waiting for the pickup." Julianna crossed her arms.

"We risked life and limb every time we went to Catlettsburg for fuel. I'm not using my gas to go work for slave wages." Shane picked up a twig and broke off small pieces to toss into the creek.

"At least we have electricity." Elizabeth seemed to be looking for a silver lining, although she'd seldom appeared as if she'd found one ever since Pastor Joel had died.

Neither Shane nor Julianna commented.

"Can you remind me, how did a woman from a gang of known drug dealers and thieves end up in the human resources department?" Julianna fumed.

"Wallace Hayes put her there." Shane threw the last length of his stick into the swirling waters below the bridge. "Probably just because he knew it would eat at us. He's limited by the ESC and unable to exact a direct retribution to get even with us, but any chance he gets to make our lives harder, you better believe he'll take it."

Finally, the bus came into view. Julianna motioned toward the vehicle. "Oh, great. We're being taken to the work camp in a school bus. This brings back memories."

Shane let Julianna and Elizabeth get on first, then climbed the stairs. The driver wore a white polo with a UN insignia, much like the one worn by Tessa. He looked at the faces of the other five workers on the bus. They all looked just as unhappy about being there as his group. Shane sat next to Julianna and the bus continued its route.

The next stop was in front of the Teague compound. Johnny, his twenty-something son, and his late-teen daughter got on the bus. Johnny took the seat in front of Shane.

"Heading out to the woods with the rest of us?"

Shane asked with a dry voice.

"Nope, taking the kids to Disneyland." Johnny turned around with a stern look. "Why? I didn't get on the wrong bus, did I?"

Julianna looked out the windows and crossed her arms tightly. "I think we're all on the wrong bus."

The vehicle took them out to the Smoky Mountain National Park where logging crews were already working. Logging roads were being cut into the sides of mountains by massive bulldozers which were laying waste to the natural beauty all around.

As they exited the bus on the side of the road, each of them was issued a pair of work gloves, a hard hat, and an orange safety vest. A tall late-fifties foreman introduced himself. "I'm Chris King. You folks will be working under me. I know most of you'd rather be doing something else, but let's try to make the best of what we have to work with in this situation.

"Real quick about me, I've worked for twenty years in forestry. I started out logging, then picked up a management job with a local maintenance crew clearing limbs for the power company. I like working with people, so I grabbed this gig when it opened up. All of us have to contribute, so I figured I might as well do something I'm familiar with. I'm not here to crack heads, but we do have a quota to meet. As long as we stay on schedule, you won't hear much out of me.

"For the most part, you folks will be taking the limbs off of the larger trees as we take them down. From there, you'll cut them up into smaller pieces and stack them in piles. Chipper crews will come to pick up those and take them to the paper plant to be manufactured into paper products."

"My advice is for y'all to work it out amongst yourselves. Those of you who know how to run a saw can do that and the rest of you can drag branches. I'll be around every two hours or so to check on you. If you think of something you need, let me know when you see me. Gas, bar-and-chain oil, water, and snacks are on the truck. Be safe."

Shane gazed at the towering hardwoods which had already been felled, leaving a path of disarray like that of an F-5 tornado. He redirected his attention to the heavy-duty work truck where the supplies were located. "Johnny, we'll work together if you want."

Johnny turned to his kids. "Looks like we ain't gonna make Disney today. Jed, you grab a chainsaw. Janie, you stick with Mrs. Hayes and drag limbs."

"Yes, sir," both answered.

Julianna selected the smallest chainsaw.

"You could pull limbs if you want." Shane pulled an orange mesh vest overtop of his shirt.

She slipped her hands into a pair of gloves. "Are you trying to get rid of me?"

A shy grin worked its way across his face. "No."

"Good." She pulled the goggles over her eyes and walked toward the nearest tree before Shane could see whether or not she was smiling also.

Shane followed her to the tree, started his saw, and began removing limbs.

Two hours later, Chris King came around. He signaled for Shane's team to turn off their saws.

Shane flipped up the toggle switch, and the saw fell silent. He removed his goggles and hard hat.

"Y'all ain't ever worked in forestry before, have you?" King asked with a smile.

"No, sir," Shane answered for the group. "It might take us a day or two to get a system going, but we'll get the hang of it."

King looked at the four trees stripped of their branches and the accompanying mountains of brush. "That's not what I meant. This is hourly work. We don't want to be lazy, but it's important to pace yourselves. What you've done would represent a day's work for most crews your size. You might want throttle back some for the rest of the day."

"Are you asking us to milk it?" Johnny wiped the sweat from his forehead.

King lowered his brows. "We don't like to use that terminology. Pace yourselves. That sounds better. Today's not as hot as it can be out here. And it's not raining. The head honchos don't take things like that into account when conditions are worse, so it's best not to set expectations too high if you catch my drift."

"We understand perfectly." Julianna cleaned her goggles with her shirttail. "So are you saying we shouldn't make any more progress for the rest of the day?"

"Go ahead and take lunch. I'll come around later and see how you're doing, but that's a pretty good first day's work."

"I know we're supposedly working for the ESC to earn our keep and provide some value for the international bailout." Jed pointed at the insignia on the work truck "But what does LSA Global Logistics have to do with it?"

"They're the ones who got the contracts for resource extraction and delivery," said King.

Janie inspected the logo. "What does LSA stand for?"

Shane answered, "Land, Sea, and Air. Maris Allard's husband is the CEO. But I'm sure that had no bearing on them getting the contract."

"I'm sure it didn't." King chuckled. "And I'm sure it has nothing to do with LSA being allowed to set the price for timber and every other commodity of value they can squeeze out of this country. Like I said, don't work yourselves to death." King walked up the freshly bulldozed dirt road.

"So now what are we supposed to do for the rest of the day?" Jed asked.

"I'm going to hydrate for one thing." Shane collected his gear and started toward the truck.

The others followed. Janie walked next to her father. "We could forage for mushrooms."

"If you pick the wrong ones, I'll be dragging limbs by myself for the rest of the week," Elizabeth Hayes joked.

"She knows what she's doin'," Johnny countered. "She finds mushrooms all over the place on our farm."

"Really? Like what?" Julianna asked.

"Oyster mushrooms, chanterelles, chicken of the woods, hen of the woods, morels from time to time." Janie turned and walked backward to reply to Julianna's inquiry. "But chants are the thing to get right now. They like it hot and moist. All this rain we've been getting makes for perfect conditions."

"Are they any good?" Shane quizzed.

"Best eatin' mushroom I've ever had," said Johnny. "Meaty with a mild flavor. They go with about anything."

"Okay, let's see what the truck has for snacks, and we'll venture out after lunch." Shane opened the back door of the truck to find a cardboard box of MREs, single-serve bags of chips, and individually wrapped snack cakes.

"We could take a few of these MREs home for a rainy day." Julianna grabbed two and inspected the contents of each.

"I might need a few of those snack cakes in case I wake up in the middle of the night," said Jed.

"Bar-and-chain oil is hard to come by, too." Johnny took two-quart bottles and stowed them in the pack he'd brought with him.

After lunch, the group meandered out into the woods in search of edible mushrooms. Shane and Julianna stayed close to Janie who acted as lead scout. "What are we looking for?" Shane asked. "Will they be growing on fallen trees?"

"No," Janie answered. "They're not dependent on decaying wood for nutrients. Chants grow symbiotically with hardwoods. So we'll be looking on the forest floor around big healthy oaks, maples, that sort of thing."

"Somebody paid attention during biology class," Julianna commented.

"Are you kidding? I went to public school," she said. "I learned all of this on my own."

"What color are they?" Shane held a sapling to help himself up a steep incline.

"Yellowish, with kind of an orange tint," Janie answered. "The more mature ones have ruffled edges, sort of like a flower petal."

Jed broke away from the group. "I think I see some over here."

Shane cut left to find Jed. He looked at several yellow fungi popping up from the forest floor.

Janie came over and picked one. She held it so Shane and Julianna could see underneath. "See how the veins fork near the edge of the cap and run down the stipe?"

"Yes," said Julianna. "Aren't those called gills?"

"In chants, they're actually called false gills. True gills run parallel and don't typically fork like that. Also, they usually terminate at the stipe. The only two things that look like them are false chanterelles and Jack-o'-lanterns. False chants probably won't make you sick if you cook them, but taste bitter. Jack-o'-lanterns will make you sick as a dog, but won't kill you. Jack-o'-lanterns grow on decaying organisms or near the roots of a dead tree. Additionally, the inside of a Jack-o'-lantern is orange." She pulled the mushroom apart down the middle. "Chants are white inside."

"Kinda looks like string cheese," Shane said.

"Exactly," confirmed Janie.

Shane picked a few and placed them in a mutual collection bag. Julianna did also. "I'm interested to see what they taste like. I hope we find enough for a nice meal."

After learning to identify the mushrooms, the

group split up into smaller teams in order to cover more ground. Julianna and Shane ventured out on their own.

Once they'd wandered far enough to be out of sight, Julianna gently put her hand in his. She interlaced her fingers between Shane's.

His heart pounded, yet he remembered the scathing rebuke that had followed his misinterpretation of the gesture previously. *Why is she doing this?* Shane thought. *Is she intentionally trying to torture me? It doesn't matter anyway. It's not like I'm going to pull my hand away from hers. If this is as good as it gets then I have no choice but to settle.*

"What are you thinking?" she asked.

"Me?" He wondered if his facial expressions had betrayed his innermost thoughts.

"Yeah, you." She laughed. "What are you thinking about this situation?"

"I…I…I… What are you thinking?"

"I don't know." She seemed pensive as they walked hand in hand. "I guess we don't stand a chance."

His stomach sank. No new revelation had come, but it still pained him to hear it verbalized. He added nothing to her statement.

She continued. "I suppose our options are to be content living as slaves or to go out in a blaze of glory, standing up for what we believe in."

Shane gave a sigh of relief at having assumed the topic of conversation was something else entirely. "Oh, yeah. Right."

She stared absently at the forest floor. "If it

wasn't for Cole, I'd have no problem choosing the latter, but the joy I get from seeing his face every day covers a multitude of misery."

"I know what you mean." Shane felt blessed to have been given a second chance at being Cole's father.

"But you must have an opinion. Let's hear it," she prodded.

"Mom, Dad, Pastor Joel, Dan, Eric, so many people have died, and we're no more free than if we'd just let Wallace Hayes have his way in the first place. It seems like a lot of sacrifice for nothing."

She swung her arm to and fro, carrying Shane's hand in the rhythm. "Maybe, but maybe not. Could we have lived with ourselves if we hadn't at least tried? If I'm beaten, okay. But I'm not the kind of girl to sit back and take it. You're not either."

"I'm not that kind of girl?" Shane grinned.

She fought a smile, squeezed his hand, and mischievously tried to pull him off balance. "You know what I mean."

He caught himself from falling by flinging his arms around her. "Yeah, I know." He pried himself away from the embrace before he lost control. Shane loved this time alone with her immensely. He only wished it were more.

She pushed him away from her, but in a playful and flirtatious way. "Look! Mushrooms!" The two of them gathered as many of the chanterelles as they could find, then continued the hunt.

CHAPTER 14

The sleep of a labouring man is sweet, whether he eat little or much: but the abundance of the rich will not suffer him to sleep.

Ecclesiastes 5:12

The weeks passed and Shane's group found a rhythm to life. They worked with the forestry program, kept up with chores around the compound, and tried to make the best of a bad situation. One late-August morning, Shane, Julianna, and Elizabeth waited at the bottom of the long gravel driveway for the bus to take them to the job site.

Shane spotted a white Jeep with UN insignia approaching. "Here comes trouble?"

Elizabeth sounded anxious. "Why do you say that?"

Julianna crossed her arms and answered for him. "They've always proved to be bearers of bad news before."

The vehicle rolled to a stop directly in front of them. The passenger's side window rolled down and a heavily tattooed arm came out with an envelope pointed like a gun at Shane.

"What's this?" Shane stepped back rather than accept the aggressively-issued letter.

"New work orders," said Tessa.

"Seriously? You're having us transferred to sanitation?" Shane wanted so badly to spit on her.

Tessa cackled. "I wish! But unfortunately, we're not there yet. For now, I'll have to settle for knowing that you're working four days a week instead of three."

"Four days a week?" Shane's brows snapped together like a pair of magnets.

"Yeah." She waved the envelope. "All the details are inside. Just take the letter. Otherwise, you'll have to take a trip downtown to get a new form. Or, you can refuse, and we'll put you in a residential work camp. Separate from your kids, of course."

Shane snatched the envelope from her hand and glared at her.

She offered a vile smirk. "Have a nice day." She rolled up her window and the Jeep pulled away.

"It's just one more day. We still have three days to do what we want." Elizabeth's voice sounded artificially soothing.

Nevertheless, Shane seethed with fury. "Then it

will be five days, then six, then ten-hour shifts, then twelve-hour shifts. Incrementalism. It's how the left gets things done. We can't let them keep pushing us further and further back into a corner."

"What are we going to do?" Julianna's face showed that she too was very perturbed over the latest development.

"I don't know." The bus pulled up to the three of them. Shane let Elizabeth and Julianna get on first. "But if we don't push back, they won't stop until they have us in a concentration camp. Especially if Wallace Hayes and Tessa have any say in it."

The bus stopped up the road and a red-faced Johnny Teague stomped up the stairs. He marched past Shane with a crumpled envelope in his hand. Janie and Jed followed their father.

Once the bus was in motion, Shane turned to Johnny. "I see you got one, too." He held up his own crinkled letter.

"It ain't gonna stop here." Johnny's handlebar mustache curved downward more dramatically than usual.

"I know." Shane took a deep breath and tried to accept the undesirable hand he'd been dealt.

"What are we going to do about it?" Johnny asked.

"I'm not sure what we can do. We're outnumbered, outgunned, and all-around outplayed."

"That ain't never stopped you before."

Shane frowned at the thought. "Yeah, but I've lived to regret it more often than not."

Johnny put his hand on Shane's shoulder. "Every

time we've lost someone, it's been the doin' of some evil devil like Harvey Hammer or Wallace Hayes. Don't put none of that on yourself. Right or wrong, you act when others are paralyzed by fear."

"I'm working on being less hasty and reckless."

"Hmm," Johnny growled. "I can understand that, but don't pitch the baby out with the bathwater. And don't confuse decisiveness with imprudence. Take your time, come up with something good, but don't just give up. We'll all be looking to you."

Shane let his eyes drift down to the rubberized flooring in the aisle of the bus. "I hate to burst your bubble, but we don't have much to work with this time."

Johnny leaned forward and addressed Julianna. "You keep encouraging him today. He'll come up with somethin'."

"He always does," she added.

***

That day, Shane went through the motions of removing tree limbs like a robot. Every idea that came to him jeopardized Cole and Julianna's safety while offering little hope of deliverance. Once his team finished their work for the day, Julianna took him by the hand. "Come on, let's walk to the creek."

He put up no resistance but had little enthusiasm about the outing. Both were quiet for the half-hour trek through the wilderness to the babbling brook where they'd visited on multiple occasions.

A large rock which overlooked the rushing

waters of the bold stream had become their usual sitting spot. Shane dangled his boots over the side. "Even if we wanted to commit ourselves to a suicide mission, we don't have the guns to do it."

"Does it have to be a suicide mission?" The outside corners of her eyes pulled down.

"Unless it's a more indirect action," he said.

"Like what?"

"Harassing the enemy. Trying to break them down."

"You mean like sabotage?"

"That's one example, sure."

"It's less risky. As long as we're smart about it and don't get caught." Her cheeks perked up.

Shane stared at the water. "We could come back out here at night. They leave all of their equipment. LSA Global has so many vehicles, and so much fuel out here, a forest fire would burn for weeks."

"Yeah!" Julianna stood up. "What was that word Creech used for hell?"

"Gehenna." Shane considered the action further.

"Forest fires are a natural occurrence. They might not even be able to tell it was arson."

"At least not until the fire burns out. By then, we'll be in phase two of our plan."

"What's phase two?"

"I don't know yet," Shane said. "But we'll need guns for it."

"Where are we going to get guns?"

"Somewhere." Shane stared at the rushing stream. "Where there's a will, there's a way."

She kissed him on the side of the cheek. "See there? Things are looking brighter already."

The hairs on his neck stood up at the sensation of her lips against his face. He completely lost track of his diabolical scheme to bring down the ESC and Maris Allard. Like a biplane caught in an updraft, he found his emotions being tossed skyward, then going into freefall. He dared not look her way. He wouldn't so much as consider that her feelings toward him had changed. The teasing and torment weighed on him like an anvil, yet he couldn't help yearning for more.

***

On the way home, Johnny asked, "Come up with anything?"

"Maybe. We could at least get some time off. But we need to take it slow. Get the entire strategy ironed out. In the meantime, we need to start working on all the other disgruntled workers. We're going to need every person we can get if this is to be anything other than a worthless bloodletting."

"I knew you'd come around." Johnny smiled and nudged Shane's shoulder with his fist.

Shane went over what they'd come up with so far. Janie and Jed listened in.

"A forest fire? That's so destructive!" Janie's eyes showed her distress.

Julianna spoke calmly. "These trees are doomed anyway. Maris Allard is determined to clear cut the entire Smoky Mountain National Park. If we can be a small part of making that business model unprofitable, perhaps some of the park can be spared."

"You're not worried about the fire spreading all the way to Sylva?" Jed inquired.

"It's been pretty wet. I can't imagine the fire getting outside of the park." Shane said. "I know it's a drastic measure, but we're in a tight spot with few options."

"What about the guns?" Johnny asked. "We have less than ten battle rifles between both of our compounds."

"The Hill Runners have guns," Julianna replied.

"True," said Shane. "But whatever we do, we're going to need their help. The Hill Runners will be using those rifles, assuming we can get their assistance."

"Who else has guns?" Johnny asked.

"The UN troops." Shane pressed his lips together.

Johnny laughed. "Yeah, right. They ain't gonna sell them to us. Not for all the gold in the world."

"Maybe not to us and maybe not for gold," Shane said.

"I'm listening." Johnny tilted his chin up.

"Alcohol is in short supply and from what I can tell, it's the primary pastime for the peacekeepers who don't see much action around these parts."

Johnny stroked the sides of his mustache. "We've got a good bit of corn in the field. I suppose we could use our measly paychecks to buy sugar from the commissary. But even so, we'd need a still. And a big one if we were going to make enough to entice the UN troops."

"I might know of a place with a still." Shane grinned. "The only thing we're missing is someone to make it."

"Grandpa used to make shine!" Janie exclaimed.

"James?" Shane looked at Johnny with surprise.

Johnny's eyes narrowed as he glared at his daughter, then he turned his attention back to Shane. "He might have made a batch or two—for medicinal purposes."

Julianna rolled her eyes. "Sounds like this part of the country has stayed pretty well medicated over the years."

"Do you think he'll do it?" Shane inquired.

"Even if he does, what's the plan?" Johnny asked. "Are you going to walk into the sheriff's department with a case of Mason jars filled with liquor?"

"No." Shane thought for a moment. "Most of the soldiers are staying at that hotel on the river in Dillsboro. Whoever approaches them will go there."

"Whoever approaches them has a good chance of getting shot," Johnny warned. "They ain't about to sell guns that they know are going to be used against them."

"Probably not, but if a couple of the Hill Runners show up with some booze and a good cover story about how they're dealing guns in Chicago, the plan just might work."

Johnny stared out the window of the bus. "Chicago is a failed city. The UN pulled out of there long ago. I suppose they wouldn't feel any moral obligation against selling guns that were going to end up there. Let me talk to Pop about it when I get home. We'll sleep on it and talk it over in the morning."

Shane nodded. "Good enough. For now, it's business as usual. We'll start working with some of the other crews instead of sticking to ourselves so much. But take it slow. Feel people out before you start outright asking them how they feel about the new four-day workweek. I'll have Bobby's group do the same."

"Sounds good," said Johnny. "I'll run it all by Jimmy this evening."

"Great." Julianna smiled. "It sounds like we've got ourselves a revolution in the making."

CHAPTER 15

First they came for the socialists, and I did not speak out—
Because I was not a socialist.

Then they came for the trade unionists, and I did not speak out—
Because I was not a trade unionist.

Then they came for the Jews, and I did not speak out—
Because I was not a Jew.

Then they came for me—and there was no one left to speak for me.

Martin Niemöller

One week later.

Sunday after service, Shane assisted Kari Ensley in hitching the trailer to the back of her truck. "We really appreciate you letting us use the still. I'm sure James will be grateful for your assistance in keeping it running through the week."

Kari checked the hitch to make sure it was secure. "What are you going to tell Rita Carmichael and her little minion, Tessa, when they ask why I didn't show up for work?"

"I'll tell them you went to stay with friends, Wyoming or somewhere."

"It's going to be awfully lonely out there with just me and Scott." Kari looked back toward the chestnut tree where everyone gathered after the sermon each week.

Shane dusted his hands off on his jeans. "Not for long. I suspect James will be out there every other day with a load of corn or sugar."

Scott came to stand by his mother's side. "Is Cole coming out to Pawpaw's?"

"Soon." Shane ran his hand across the young boy's head. "Probably in about a month." He knelt down and looked Scott in the eyes. "Hopefully we'll get all this straightened out, and we won't have to be going back and forth so often."

"I don't mind. I just wish Cole could come with us."

"You're a brave boy. You be good for your

mama and help out as much as you can."

"With making the medicine, you mean?" Scott asked for clarification.

"Yeah." Shane stood up with a grin. "With making the medicine."

Julianna and Angela came to the trailer area as Kari was getting into the truck. Each carried a large cardboard box which they placed in the bed of the truck. Julianna said, "Here are some more MREs and snack cakes we've brought home from work."

"We'll never eat all of that," Kari said.

"I know," said Angela. "But we need to start getting as many supplies out there as we can if it's going to be our fallback position."

Shane closed the door for Scott after he'd entered the passenger's side of the cab. "We'll come out next Sunday evening with some supplies. We'll plan to stay for a visit to keep you company."

"Thanks." Kari started the ignition.

"Will you bring Cole?" Scott inquired.

Shane grinned. "We'll bring Cole when we come next week."

Kari pulled away with her trailer in tow. James and Jimmy drove a second pickup truck behind her. They were taking a load of corn out to Pawpaw's to begin the fermentation process and also acting as an escort for Kari to make sure she had no trouble on the short trip to Murphy.

Shane walked with Julianna and Angela back to the potluck gathering. Elizabeth Hayes was assisting Betty Teague with putting away the leftovers. Bobby sat at the picnic table with Johnny and his son Jed. Shane put his hand on Bobby's shoulder. "You ready to roll out, big guy?"

"Let's go." Bobby stood.

"You be safe." Julianna grabbed the tip of his fingers but let his hand drop away almost immediately.

"I will. It's just a quick drive up to Maggie. We'll be back before dark." He waited to see if she'd offer a hug, but Julianna gave no indication of any such intention.

"Bye, Shane." Cole hugged his waist.

Shane bent down to embrace his son. "Bye, bye. I know we usually hang out together all day on Sunday. I'll try to make it up to you Tuesday. I've been seeing some big shellcrackers in the pond. Maybe we'll take some poles down there early on Tuesday morning and see if we can pull out some dinner. Then we can go look for mushrooms up on the trail. We'll have a big feast waiting for Bobby and Angela when they get home from work."

"Yeah!" Cole agreed. "We could get a mess of frogs to go with the fish, too!"

"Good plan." Shane hugged him tight, then walked to the truck with Bobby at his side.

The two of them were on the road in a matter of minutes. Bobby looked over from the passenger's seat of the Ram. "What are you going to do if Wrench says no?"

"Go to plan B."

"What's plan B?"

"I'm not dedicating any thought to plan B until plan A fails."

"I'm just saying, it's kind of a long shot."

"How so?"

Bobby raised his shoulders. "The Hill Runners are relatively safe at the moment. They don't have a dog in this fight. Plus, Wrench lost his wingman in the last skirmish."

"We'll have to make it worth their while."

"With what?"

"I'll have to find out what they need and then figure out a way to get it for them."

"You haven't dedicated much thought to plan A either, have you?"

"Kind of making it up as I go along."

Shane pulled up to Wrench's garage a half an hour later.

Five bikers with AK-47s walked up to the truck.

"They seem to be making good use of the guns we took from the Iron Devils." Shane recognized one of the bikers and waved at him. "Colin, hey. Is Wrench around?"

The heavy man wore an American flag bandana around long black hair and had a full beard. "Shane. Good to see you, man." Colin motioned for the other men to lower their weapons. "He's in the shop working on somethin'."

Shane and Bobby stepped out of the truck slowly so not to make anyone nervous. They followed him inside where they found Wrench with a welding mask over his face and a torch in his hand. Wrench flipped up his mask, turned off his torch, stood up, and wiped his hands on his greasy coveralls before offering to shake with Shane. "How have you boys been?"

"Could be better," Shane shook his hand firmly.

Wrench hung his welding mask on the

handlebars of the bike he'd been working on. "I heard. You've got the UN running things down in Jackson County. Not all it's cracked up to be?"

"Not at all." Shane shook his head. "They've got us all working at a forced labor program. We're clear-cutting the Smoky Mountain National Park."

"Well, you've got job security. That's about a half-million acres of forest isn't it?"

Bobby nodded. "Yeah, we've got more trees than we've got patience for dealing with being treated like slaves."

"Which is why we're here," Shane added. He explained the recent increase in work demands and provided a rough draft of his plan to put an end to the LSA Global operations in the area.

Wrench listened without interrupting. "I can certainly understand why you're upset. But we're all still a little gun shy from the last operation. Besides, taking on peacekeepers with armored vehicles is an entirely different animal from ambushing a ring of drunk bikers in the middle of the night. I empathize with your situation, but it wouldn't be in our best interest. If we can do anything else to help out that doesn't involve getting into a shootout with the ESC or the UN, let me know. I always like to help—when I can."

"Eventually, the people in Jackson County will wise up. If slavery is the best we can hope for, we'll pack up and get out of town."

"Where will you go?" Wrench asked.

"Anywhere the ESC isn't implementing a forced labor program. Then guess where LSA Global will start looking for a cheap workforce?"

Wrench grimaced and turned to his bike.

Shane continued his lecture. "Only when they get here, they'll know better than to let their workforce go home at night. They'll build fences with gates, and towers with guards."

Wrench muttered, "No straw for your bricks."

"You're starting to get the picture," Shane replied.

"But suppose we make conditions bad for business in Jackson County," Wrench speculated. "We may serve only to hasten the demise of our own freedom."

"That's not the way I see it shaking out," said Shane. "But if the worst were to happen, you can count on us. We'll be right by your side until it's over, no matter the outcome."

"I don't like it." Wrench squatted down beside his project. "Especially this idea of having one of my guys waltz into the hotel where the peacekeepers are staying with a jug of shine."

"I'm open to suggestions. What do you recommend we do to make the plan better?"

"It would be much better if there were a bar. Neutral territory. It makes a much more likely location for a supposed chance encounter such as you've envisioned."

"A bar." Shane thought for a moment. "Okay. The Teagues know just about everyone in town. I'm sure they can find someone who can facilitate some type of watering hole opening up."

"Now wait a minute." Wrench turned from his work. "I'm not saying we'd be willing to get involved. I'm just offering a hypothetical solution."

Shane held up his hand. "I know. I'm just thinking your solution through—hypothetically."

Bobby turned to Shane. "Even if the Hill Runners were to assist us in the acquisition of firearms through our pop-up cantina, that wouldn't necessarily bind them to being involved in any direct action, would it?"

"Not at all," Shane said.

Bobby motioned toward Wrench. "The Hill Runners would be entitled to some percentage of the transactions wouldn't they?"

"Twenty percent," Shane replied.

"Fifty," Wrench countered.

"Twenty-five."

Wrench stood up. "Forty."

"Thirty."

"Thirty-five." Wrench tightened his jaw. "We're taking on a lot of risk getting involved in this thing at all. That's the lowest we can go."

"One third. You can take one-third of the shine that we provide for the operation. Plus, if you can manage to swindle a finder's fee out of the peacekeepers, then more power to you." Shane extended his hand.

Wrench's hard mouth line slowly melted into a grin. He embraced Shane's hand. "Deal!"

***

The next morning, Johnny Teague, his son, and daughter got onto the bus. As usual, Johnny sat directly behind Shane and Julianna. "How did your meeting go?"

"Could have been better," Shane shifted sideways in his seat.

Julianna also pivoted to face Johnny. "Could have been worse."

"The good news is that the Hill Runners have committed to helping us acquire weapons," Shane said with little enthusiasm.

"What's the bad news?" Johnny asked.

"They won't commit to being involved in any direct action."

"Yet," Julianna added.

"That's not all." Shane's eyebrows sank. "They want a bar set up, to make the initial contact with the peacekeepers seem more natural."

"This is becoming a fairly elaborate scheme," said Johnny.

Julianna put her hand on the back of the seat. "Revolutions usually are. At least the successful ones, anyway."

"Mandy, Jimmy's wife, she knows the Campbells. They own the Old Mill Bar. I suppose she could talk to them about re-opening." Johnny stroked the handles of his mustache. "They might do it. Especially if they're going to have some product to move."

"Yeah, but make sure they understand that we'll be setting the price and regulating the flow. They're welcome to operate at a profit if they can, but their primary motivation should be assisting us with the cause," said Shane.

"Will do," Johnny agreed. "What extra day are y'all picking up?"

Julianna answered, "Shane is picking up

Tuesday, and I'm picking up Thursday. Plus Shane will be switching Friday for Saturday. That way one of us is at home with Cole on the days Angela works."

Johnny shook his head. "They really threw a wrench in the works for us by adding that extra day."

"If we don't pull this off, it'll soon be a six-day workweek." Shane looked out the window at the mountains in the distance. "Then we'll really be up the creek."

CHAPTER 16

It does not take a majority to prevail... but rather an irate, tireless minority, keen on setting brushfires of freedom in the minds of men.

Samuel Adams

The weeks passed with Shane's group making steady progress toward their aim. Many of the other conscripted laborers from Jackson County joined their ranks.

One late September Wednesday evening, Shane returned home from his work with the logging crew. He collected some clean clothes from his trailer and went to the cabin to take a shower. He knocked before entering.

"Come in," called Angela.

He entered to see his sister, Julianna, and Cole all gathered around the television. "We've got TV!"

"We've got PBS." Julianna didn't turn away from the television.

"How?" He stared at the odd sight of the television being anything other than a dust collector.

"I'm using my phone as a hot spot for the Roku," she replied.

His eyes widened. "You've got internet on your phone?"

"It's been going in and out all day, but yeah. I suppose the government is supporting internet-based television providers like Roku and Apple TV."

"What websites are working?" He placed his clothes on the kitchen counter and sat down on one of the bar stools.

"Google is up but no email service yet. None of the big e-commerce sites are working. I suppose we'd have to have delivery services before any of them could be viable," Julianna replied.

"How is it possible for Google to be up and running?" Shane inquired. "Without companies to purchase ads, they can't possibly stay solvent. Besides, isn't San Francisco considered a failed city by the ESC?"

Julianna glanced up momentarily from the television. "San Francisco proper is, but evidently the UN has cordoned off the areas they view as being worth saving. They've erected fences around Palo Alto and Mountain View."

Shane nodded. "Concentration camps."

"Maybe so, but PBS has been showing footage all day of people clambering to get inside the new sanctuary zone." Julianna sat on the futon with her arm around Cole.

Shane knitted his eyebrows together. "Sanctuary zone?"

"Food, water, security." Angela looked at her brother. "People outside the fence have none of those things."

Julianna added, "And about Google's finances, the ESC is footing the bill. Google is essentially the backbone of the internet now, so I suppose they qualify as a public utility which makes them a target for being nationalized."

"Are we still calling it that? Nationalized, I mean." Angela pulled her hair behind her ear. "After all, we don't really have a national identity anymore."

"How about Globalized?" Shane suggested.

Julianna stroked Cole's forehead with her thumb. "Very fitting. I'm sure the UN will like it. Why don't you drop it in the suggestion box at work?"

"I've got a few other recommendations for them if we ever get a suggestion box." Shane picked up his clothes from the counter. "I'm going to get a quick shower. Let me know if PBS has anything important to say."

"Oh, I've got a full news brief for you when you get out," said Julianna.

Shane hurried to get his shower so he could hear the latest news. He came out of the bathroom as soon as he had his jeans on. He listened from the hallway while the PBS anchorwoman delivered the latest events with a modicum of zeal.

"The SDR has stabilized against gold and the new gold-backed RNB. While the IMF's cryptocurrency is still vying for favor in the east, it has achieved widespread acceptance in Western Europe and the Americas.

"Economists are crediting the surge in confidence for the SDR to the rapid success which the Economic Stability Commission is achieving in the United States' renaissance cities. The list of metropolitan areas which are having utilities restored is growing by the day. Palo Alto, California; Huntington, West Virginia; Lexington, Kentucky; Traverse City, Michigan; Camden, Maine; Taos, New Mexico; and Colorado Springs all have internet service, cell service, water, fire, EMS, and police services restored. Gas stations and grocery stores are coming back on line and curfews have been extended to midnight. These renaissance cities are proof that the ESC's plan is working. In a public forum yesterday, Maris Allard stated that she hopes to double the number of functioning renaissance cities before the end of the year.

"The rest of the world is watching and it appears the global economy may be emerging from the catastrophic depression brought on by the failure of the US dollar. We are seeing global trade beginning to resume in certain markets."

"Oil prices continue to stay at astronomical levels as OPEC insists on gold settlement. This resistance to get on board with the new global currency by the cartel has forced many nations to rely solely on domestically-produced petroleum products. Many speculators believe OPEC will have to relent or face being stuck with a glut of product for which there is no market. For the time being, central banks are stepping in to convert SDRs to gold for imported oil settlement. However, this practice is being reserved for critical demand when adequate fuel supplies are absolutely necessary and not merely an inconvenience."

Shane dried his hair and let the towel hang around his neck. "Renaissance cities. I wonder who came up with that one."

Julianna looked over the back of the futon. "It sounds a little optimistic if you ask me. It assumes we've already weathered the fall of Rome and survived the brutality and plagues of the Dark Ages."

Angela said, "I know, right? It's been less than a year since the collapse."

Shane continued, "Remember what Dad used to say, this is all a confidence game. PBS is part of the propaganda machine responsible for getting everyone to accept the SDR. Notice how they've stopped reporting on the madness and mayhem in all the major cities in the countries. The UN and ESC know the best they can hope for is to let the population centers die-off and burnout like a bad virus. But nothing about that story instills confidence in the currency."

"Did you notice that Huntington, West Virginia was listed as one of the ESC's examples of shining success?" Julianna asked.

"Mmmhmm." Shane took his towel and hung it on the hook behind the bathroom door. "The amount of bribes and corruption holding that operation together is unprecedented. Lots of money and favors flowing in both directions between Caleb Creech and the ESC administrators. Neither of them likes the other, so it's a tinderbox which could go up in flames at any moment.

"We're in the loop on Huntington because of our business dealings with Creech. For all we know, the other so-called renaissance cities could be little more than card houses held together with tape and paper clips."

A knock came to the door.

Julianna whispered, "Cole, go to the back bedroom."

"Mama?" His eyes showed his distress.

"It's okay. I'll come with you," Angela sprung from the couch and took Cole's hand.

Shane pulled his tee-shirt over his head and looked out the peephole. "It's Mandy Teague."

"All clear," Julianna called to Angela and Cole.

Shane opened the door. "Hey, Mandy. Come on in."

"Sorry to pop by unannounced." She stepped inside.

Julianna pushed her hands into her jean pockets. "That's okay. What's up?"

"It's Ed and Liz Campbell," she said.

"From the bar?" Shane asked.

"Yes." Mandy seemed to hesitate when Angela walked back into the room. "Greg stopped by last night."

Shane glanced at his sister. "In his capacity as the assistant constable?"

"Deputy Constable," Mandy corrected. "That's what he calls himself, anyway. He says the Old Mill can't stay open without a liquor license and a business license."

"But they have all of that! I don't understand what the problem is." Shane scowled.

"Greg says the fees haven't been paid for this year." Mandy lifted her shoulders.

"The city isn't set up to accept SDRs yet and the ESC hasn't provided a way for local businesses to get paid using SDRs either," Julianna complained. "Our pittance is paid to us each week on the ESC app via our phones. It's capped at 100 SDRs worth of transfers per day. A business couldn't operate like that."

"I'm guessing Hayes is looking for a shakedown. That's his MO," said Shane.

"Yeah, but how are they going to make ends meet if they have to shell out all their revenues to Hayes?" Mandy asked. "They have to be able to pay workers, even if the booze is being donated by the cause."

Angela seemed not to be upset by the mention of her derelict husband. "What if a famous country music performer were to be on stage at the Old Mill? That might be a draw. At least enough to keep Wallace Hayes paid off."

"I'm a guitar player. I don't sing," said Shane.

"Julianna sings." Angela smiled. "Like an angel."

"Yeah, well, angels don't sing about the smut

written in Backwoods' songs." Julianna crossed her arms. "Not even for a good cause."

"What about some of the older classics?" Angela asked. "Country used to have songs that weren't about cheating, drinking, and fornication. I'm sure you two could put together a set."

"I would still be performing in a bar." She kept her arms crossed tight.

"The bar which is the key to getting the ESC and UN out of Jackson County," said Mandy.

Julianna sighed.

Shane looked at her. "What do you think?"

Her brows lowered as if in thought. "I suppose."

"Good!" Shane turned to Mandy. "Have the Campbells go down to Hayes' office and see what it would take to get all of their licenses up-to-date. We'll get something figured out."

"We've got one other small hiccup," said Mandy.

"These small hiccups are beginning to pile up," Shane replied. "What's the problem?"

"The peacekeepers. They're starting to hear about the bar. Some came in last night, but they don't have silver coin to trade with. All they have is SDRs and 7.62 rounds. Since it's illegal to have guns and ammo, Ed and Liz can't really accept bullets for drinks."

"We're in the mountains. We have to know someone who hoards silver coins," said Shane.

"Brady Watkins would be a good place to start. Pop said people at the bank used to talk about him back in the late sixties. They said he'd come in every day to cash in dollars for rolls of quarters and dimes."

"Brady Watkins." Shane tried to put a face to the name. "Is he the ornery old mountain goat who was elected as a county commissioner?"

"The one and only," Mandy replied.

Shane asked, "Do you know where he lives?"

"Somewhere off Sutton Branch," Mandy said. "Pop can tell you exactly."

Shane said, "They stopped minting dimes and quarters with silver in 1964. The late sixties is when people started collecting them for the precious metal value. I'm off work tomorrow. I'll take Cole up to his place after breakfast if you'll get directions for me."

"I'll get directions for you, but make sure he hears you coming. I guarantee he still has a shotgun or two sitting around. If he thinks you're the UN coming to get his shotgun, he may decide he's going out in a blaze of glory."

Angela said, "Even if you get the coins, how will you transfer them to the soldiers?"

"I'll have one of Wrench's boys to act as an intermediary. Trading silver dimes for ammo will be a good ice breaker. That will warm the peacekeepers up to doing business with the Hill Runners."

"Great," said Mandy. "We've got about twenty aspects of this plan that have to go perfectly in order for it to work."

"Any one of them failing could send it into a tailspin," Shane added. "And that would be the end of it all."

"No," said Julianna. "We can't think like that. If some piece of the plan doesn't work out, we'll go back to the drawing board, improvise, or whatever we have to do." She put her hand on Cole's shoulder. "This plan has got to work."

***

The following Friday night, Shane strummed his guitar at the Old Mill. He played several bluesy melodies while waiting for Julianna to show up. The tables around the stage were empty but every stool at the bar was occupied by an off-duty peacekeeper.

Ed Campbell, the bar's owner, walked up to Shane. "Thanks for coming. I think you being here will really help business."

"I appreciate what you are doing. Looks like you've got a few patrons. Did you get everything worked out with the mayor?"

"Yeah. He wants one hundred dollars in silver coin per month. So, at a dime a drink, that means our first thousand pours go straight to Wallace Hayes."

"It's a small price to pay to have him smoothing things over for us with the UN. If he has any pull at all with Rita Carmichael, he'll make sure you keep your doors open."

"Yeah. We just gotta stay focused on why we're here in the first place," Campbell sighed. "I'll let you get back to playing. Let me know if you need anything."

"I will. Thanks." Shane resumed playing. He watched as Colin and another of the Hill Runners walked into the bar. The two of them squeezed in at different places at the bar. Each bought a drink and walked toward the stage. Colin dropped four silver dimes into Shane's glass tip jar then continued past him to sit at a table with his colleague. Shane noticed the attention Colin and the other biker had garnered from the peacekeepers by throwing around silver coins.

Three girls Shane knew from high school came in next. They chatted up the peacekeepers until one of the off-duty soldiers had bought them a round of drinks. Then, one of them, Tara Becket, came to talk to Shane. "Hey, I heard you were back in town."

"Yep. Nashville melted down almost as fast as New York."

Shane continued to strum softly while he conversed with the girl who'd been a cheerleader many years ago.

She'd have never given Shane the time of day back in high school, but now she acted like an adoring fan. "That's right! You were in Times Square when those riots broke out! I saw you on TV." She put her hand on his back. "I'm so sorry about your fiancée. I heard what happened."

Shane recalled the terrible event. "Thanks."

"But you look good." She bit her lip. "Healthy I mean. Like you're getting along okay and everything."

"Thanks. You look good also."

She twirled her hair around her finger and stepped closer to him. "You know, after Backwoods started being on the radio all the time, I'd always think about how we went to school together but never really got to know each other and…"

"Hey, I'm here." Julianna came up on the stage. She eyed Tara like a cat watching a squirrel.

Tara smiled at Julianna. Her eyes darted to Shane then back to Julianna.

"This is Tara. She went to school with us," said Shane.

Julianna didn't smile. "I remember."

"Julianna, right?" asked Tara.

"Yeah," Julianna replied.

Tara grinned nervously at Shane. "Okay then. Good seeing you. Come say hi if you get a break."

"Okay, good seeing you." He continued strumming softly.

"What was that all about?" Julianna put her hands on her hips.

"A girl from school stopping by to say hello."

"Come say hi? Good seeing you? Sounded like more than that."

"Did I do something wrong?" he asked.

"No, Shane, you didn't do anything wrong! You're free to do whatever you want and talk to whoever you like." She dropped the folder containing her song sheets for the evening. The papers went everywhere. "That's what you've always done anyway, so no need to change now."

"Excuse me? Look, I've apologized over and over. I can't change the past, and I'm doing everything I know to do for the present. And furthermore, not that I have any interest in Tara Becket, but you've made it abundantly clear that there will never be anything between us. If something has changed, let me know."

She swept up the scattered song sheets and stuffed them back in the folder. "You know what? You look like you've got this covered. Why don't you do tonight's show by yourself?" Julianna scurried toward the door. "I don't want to get in the way of you living your life."

He leaned the guitar against the wall and chased her into the parking lot. He caught her before she got inside her truck. "Julianna."

She wouldn't look at him but he could see that she was crying.

"Has something changed?" He held her hand, not letting her leave.

She said nothing and concealed her tears.

"Julianna, I'm here for you. For whatever you need me to be. A friend, someone to help raise Cole, something more. You name it. Whatever you want me to be."

She held his hand and gently ran her thumb across the top of his fingers. Still, she would not look at him. "Nothing has changed. I'm sorry. I'm trying to drag you down into the hole of misery where I'm at; unable to forgive, yet unable to move on. I suppose I'm trying to punish you. It's not fair. You're right. You've apologized, and I can't ask you to do anything more than what you're doing. The only thing I can do is let you go. At least one of us should be free to live their life." She pulled her hand away. "Goodbye, Shane."

He stood speechless and watched her get into the truck and drive away. With his heart ripped to shreds, he had no other outlet than his guitar. He returned to the bar, picked up his instrument, and did his best to exorcise the horrible feelings coursing through his soul and spirit.

Shane played every sorrowful ballad he knew for the next few hours. He noticed the interactions between the peacekeepers and the Hill Runners at the corner table throughout the night. His intricate plan was coming together, but he felt no joy in it.

"Shane Black, live in concert," said a familiar voice. "What brings you out to such a seedy establishment?"

He looked up to see Wallace Hayes standing in front of him with a drink in hand. "Catharsis." Shane looked back down at the strings of his guitar and ignored the obnoxious politician in front of him.

"Talk about a reversal of fortune," Hayes mocked. "Imagine going from the Grand Ol' Opry to the grand Old Mill. I'm surprised you still have the energy to come play for us after shuckin' logs all day. But I hear it doesn't pay well, so I guess you have to do what has to be done to get by."

Shane refused to look up. He had a mission to focus on.

However, it was a totally unrelated insult which threatened to push Shane over the edge that evening. Two songs later, he looked up to see Angela's estranged husband, Greg, walking in the door of the Old Mill, and who should be on his arm but the tattooed beauty herself, Tessa. Shane felt his face get red. He considered calling it a night and smashing the guitar over Greg's head. Yet once again, he pushed his rage down for the sake of the mission at hand.

Tessa glanced over at Shane with a contemptuous smile, as if being sure to rub it in. Greg, however, avoided eye contact with Shane at all costs. Shane watched Greg order, then fumble to pick up his glass from the bar without his missing pinky. Shane resisted the urge to grin yet took some solace in the permanent inconvenience he'd bestowed upon his dirty rat of a brother-in-law.

Then, during Shane's last set of the evening, something happened which would certainly tip the scales in the coming conflict. Commander Abdulov walked in with two of his men. The other peacekeepers moved back from the bar and made a space for Abdulov. The commander placed some silver coins on the bar and ordered three shots of Pop's secret recipe.

Shane watched with anticipation, not knowing if Abdulov's presence at the Old Mill was an omen of fortune or fright. Would he tighten the reins and keep the other peacekeepers from openly trading with the Hill Runners or would he, himself be the man to provide the weapons and ammunition for his own demise? Shane finished his set, packed up his guitar, and left without saying anything to anyone.

CHAPTER 17

And say to the forest of the south, Hear the word of the Lord; Thus saith the Lord God; Behold, I will kindle a fire in thee, and it shall devour every green tree in thee, and every dry tree: the flaming flame shall not be quenched, and all faces from the south to the north shall be burned therein.

Ezekiel 20:47

Two weeks later, Shane played solo once more while he waited for Julianna to arrive at the Old Mill.

Abdulov had become a faithful patron during the fortnight prior. The commander and one of his top men walked over to Shane. "Is the girl coming tonight?" asked the commander.

"Julianna? Yeah. She should be here soon."

"Good. The music is kind of depressing when it's just you, by yourself. Don't get me wrong. Obviously, you are talented, but it's not a popular style in Kazakhstan. Can you play some more like pop music? Maybe like two or three songs?"

His comrade said, "Commander, this guy was like big-time country music star before collapse. TV, radio, everything."

"No kidding!" Abdulov sipped his drink.

Shane nodded. "That's a bygone life. However, I don't know any pop songs."

"That's okay. I didn't know you were a big shot." He took another drink and stared at Shane. "You're the guy we locked up when we first arrived, right?"

"Yes, sir."

"No hard feelings?" Abdulov offered his hand.

Shane forced a smile and shook the commander's hand. "None at all. You were just doing your job."

Abdulov dropped four silver dimes in Shane's tip jar. "Maybe you can learn a pop song or two."

Genuinely amused by the man, one side of Shane's mouth turned up. "Thank you, but country music classics are sort of our repertoire."

Abdulov left Shane to go sit next to Colin. Shane watched as he placed a box of ammo on the table for which Colin handed him a roll of silver dimes.

Julianna was setting up her song sheets when Shane turned around.

"Looks like your little plan is coming together,"

she said.

"We'll see. Tonight is the night the well runs dry. Ed and Liz only have four quarts of shine. They figure they'll run out by eight o'clock. Then, Colin will mention to one of the peacekeepers that he knows a guy who knows a guy."

She glanced over at the biker and the commander who were both laughing and drinking. "He seems to be getting along rather splendidly with Abdulov. I hope he's not forgetting which side he's on."

"Let's pray that Colin is just a really good actor." Shane pressed his lips together.

Julianna looked up at the bar where Tara Becket and her group were successfully getting peacekeepers to buy them drinks. "Once the well goes dry, I suppose the Old Mill won't need entertainers. This might be the last chance you get to say something to Tara."

"What?" Shane lowered his eyebrows. "Why would I talk to her?"

"I don't know. I kinda crashed the party the first night we were supposed to play here. I got all emotional, scared her off. She *is* pretty."

"She's also the kind of girl who hangs out in a bar."

"Lilith hung out in bars, didn't she?"

"I'm a different person than I was when I was with Lilith. Besides, meeting someone else isn't even on my radar right now. My priorities are taking care of Cole, and as much as you'll let me, looking after you. It's not your fault, Julianna, but I'm not moving on. If being Cole's father and your friend is as good as it gets, then I'll take it. I don't even deserve that, so I'll count my blessings for getting to have any relationship with you at all."

Her eyes became glossy and she turned away quickly. "Okay." She let her hair fall in her face, obscuring her eyes from Shane's view.

Shane started strumming the chords to Ring of Fire. "Are you ready?"

Julianna placed her lyric sheet on the stand and nodded.

***

The following Monday, Johnny Teague stepped onto the bus and took his usual seat behind Shane and Julianna. "Did they take the bait?" Jed sat in front of Shane and Janie sat beside her father.

"I talked to Wrench last night. We've already got five AKs." Shane sat sideways in his seat.

"That was fast."

"Colin is telling them that the opportunity is open for a limited time."

"What's the supposed reasoning for the Old Mill not being able to get liquor?"

Julianna answered, "Gangsters in Chicago and New Jersey are purchasing as much as can be produced, and at very high prices."

"Which is the same reason the window of opportunity to buy shine from the Hill Runners is so narrow," Shane added.

"The news is saying that international trade is resuming. Won't they be able to purchase booze from overseas soon?" Janie inquired.

"What PBS says to boost confidence doesn't

always align perfectly with reality. No one knows that better than the UN troops," said Shane. "Even if imported liquor becomes available, they'll have to spend money from their pay to buy it. As it stands, they're trading for guns, which they confiscated or requisitioned at no cost to themselves."

"Yeah, but couldn't they sell that stuff on the black market?" Jed asked.

"For silver coins or gold, I suppose. But it's not like they can get paid in SDRs," Shane replied. "At least not in any significant quantities."

"How many fighters do we have?" Julianna addressed Johnny.

Johnny's eyes rolled toward the ceiling, as if tallying up the numbers in his head. "About 60. Do you think the Hill Runners will reconsider fighting with us?"

"I've been prodding Wrench. I think he'll come around. If so, that will give us an extra 25 shooters." Shane looked out the window at the fall colors which painted the surrounding landscape in vivid hues of yellow, orange and red.

"Jimmy thinks Abdulov only has about 75 men. He's running three shifts with roughly 20 peacekeepers per shift. 75 accounts for days off," said Johnny.

"75?" Julianna sounded surprised. "When they first rolled in he had at least 150 troops with him."

Johnny replied, "Jimmy thinks that was in case of resistance. Jackson County has probably been reclassified as a minimal threat since the ESC's arrival. The UN probably reallocated those troops to areas perceived to be more hostile."

"With a good surprise attack, we should be able to wipe them out with minimum casualties on our end," Shane said. "If all continues as planned, we should be ready to execute the plan in two weeks."

***

On October 28th, the day Shane's group had labeled as D-day finally arrived. Shane went to work with LSA Global just as he'd done for the past three months. He did his job exactly as he'd always done, only on this occasion, he made mental notes of where each piece of machinery had been left, as well as every stack of logs to be picked up and taken to be sold. He finished his shift and returned home where he found Bobby and Julianna preparing for the assault scheduled to take place that evening.

"Welcome home." Bobby sat on the front porch loading AK-47 magazines with rounds of ammunition.

"I hope you didn't wear yourself out." Sitting on the porch swing, Julianna stuffed magazines into the pockets of a load-carrying vest which she'd managed to keep from confiscation.

"We never do more than two hours of work. I'm more rested than I would be if I were doing chores around the farm." Shane sat on the swing next to Julianna.

"Angela, Elizabeth, and Cole all left to go to the still early this morning," Julianna said.

"Good. Did you tell Cole that I love him and that I'll see him soon?"

"I told him." She took his hand. "He said he'd

miss you."

"Did Angela take the little wooden box with the coins?"

"She did." Julianna released his fingers to return to her task of readying her gear for the mission. "Betty Teague and Mandy took the young kids from their compound out there also. They have shotguns and rifles. I feel like Cole is in pretty good hands."

"As always, you're welcome to sit this one out," said Shane. "All the other moms are staying with their kids."

"I know. But this is what I'm supposed to do." She ran the tip of her finger over the edge of his fingernail ever so gently.

"Okay then." Shane looked at Bobby. "The three of us will leave at sunset to go out to the job site. We'll start the fire, then boogie back to town. We'll meet up with the Hill Runners at the hotel and clear out as many of the UN troops as we can. The bar has been closed for two days due to being unable to obtain alcohol, so they'll probably be partying on the pool deck. Johnny and Jimmy will hit the sheriff's department. Whichever team finishes first will go assist the other in mopping up."

"I'm ready to get this over with." Julianna held a bottle of Teflon oil over the bolt of her AK and squeezed several drops onto all the moving parts of the weapon.

***

Later that evening, Shane, Julianna, and Bobby arrived at the job site deep inside the Smoky

Mountain National Park. Shane stepped out of the Ram and quietly closed the door.

"Do you see anyone?" Julianna whispered.

"No," Shane replied in a hushed tone.

Bobby asked softly, "Why are we whispering?"

"Because," said Julianna. "That's what you do when you're up to no good."

Shane scanned the area with the beam of his flashlight. "Bobby, bring the bolt cutters. We'll take all the saws and anything of value from the supply truck."

Shane and Julianna stood guard while Bobby popped the lock of the truck. Afterward, they carted eight chainsaws, several quarts of bar-and-chain oil, a case of two-cycle engine oil, two cases of MREs and a cardboard box stocked with individually wrapped snack cakes to the Ram.

"What about the gas cans?" Bobby asked as he dropped two saws in the bed of the truck.

Shane slid the MREs to the rear of the bed. "We'll use the gas as an accelerant for the log stacks."

Julianna directed the beam of her flashlight to the fading fall foliage overhead. "It's a shame to have to burn it down at this time of the year."

"I agree," Shane pushed her light toward the ground. "But don't point your light up like that. It will carry for miles."

"Oh, sorry," she said.

The three of them retrieved the gas cans and doused the logs which had been harvested from the surrounding forest.

Next, Shane crawled under the supply truck and

cut the fuel line, allowing the gas to flow freely onto the ground. "Time to light them up." He handed a box of kitchen matches to each of his teammates. "Strike and drop. No time to watch the pretty flames. We need to get down the hill, back to the truck, and on with the second part of tonight's mission."

Shane struck the first match and tossed it toward the gas-soaked timber. The fuel caught the blaze instantly. Julianna hurried to the next equipment truck while Bobby hustled toward a bucket truck. Soon, flames lit up the entire hillside.

Shane frowned at the dastardly deed. He saw that one of the fires was already licking the low branches of a nearby cedar tree. "I hope this plan works. I would hate for this beautiful forest to be destroyed in vain."

"It's going to work." Julianna put her hand on his back. "Come on. Let's get out of here."

Shane turned away from the vulgar sight of the sin he'd just committed. "Okay." He took the keys out of his pocket and got into the cab of his Ram.

By the time Shane was back on the road, the brightly-burning fires were already beginning to glow against the sparse clouds in the night sky.

CHAPTER 18

I will call on the Lord, who is worthy to be praised: so shall I be saved from mine enemies. When the waves of death compassed me, the floods of ungodly men made me afraid. The sorrows of hell compassed me about; the snares of death prevented me. In my distress I called upon the Lord, and cried to my God: and he did hear my voice out of his temple, and my cry did enter into his ears.

2 Samuel 22:4-7

Shane cut the headlights as he approached the rally point up the river from the hotel. Shane drove slowly into the abandoned train yard watching for Wrench or any of the other Hill Runners.

"Over there!" Julianna pointed to a derailed boxcar which appeared to have been repurposed as some sort of work shed. "I thought I saw someone."

Shane cut the engine and stepped out of the truck cautiously. He offered the quiet whistle which had been designated as the challenge for his group. The whistle went from a high pitch, to low, then back to high. The designated reply came from behind the boxcar in the form of a whistle which went from low, to high, then back to low.

"That's them. Come on." Shane zipped up his tactical vest and slung his AK over his shoulder. Julianna and Bobby followed. Once he came around the back of the boxcar, Shane recognized many of the Hill Runners.

Wrench shook hands with Shane. "Everything go alright out at the park?"

Shane felt a twinge of guilt for what he'd done at the job site. "As well as could be expected." He looked around at the familiar faces. "Where's Colin?"

"Don't know." Wrench's face looked concerned.

"That's not the kind of answer which instills confidence," said Julianna.

"What do you want me to say?" Wrench replied. "He was supposed to meet us at the garage an hour before departure and never showed up. We even hung around for an extra fifteen minutes to see if he'd show."

Shane looked at Bobby, then Julianna, before finally turning his attention back to Wrench. "Do you think he'd sell us out?"

"I don't think he'd sell out the people from his own club," Wrench said. "He's been with us for over ten years."

"What do you want to do?" Bobby asked. "Do you think we should call off the strike?"

"We've spent months putting this together. I don't want to scrap the entire operation because we can't find one guy." Shane thought for a moment. "Colin has had his hand in the cookie jar with no oversight for the past month. I expect he's managed to siphon off a little here and there. He probably decided to leave the casino while he's winning. Maybe he's skimmed a little more than I think. Perhaps he's squirreled away enough to get out of dodge and start over somewhere. Who knows?" Shane looked at Julianna. "What do you think?"

She raised her shoulders. "I don't know. It does seem a little overly paranoid to ditch the whole mission."

"Yeah, but if he did squeal, we could be walking into a trap," said Bobby.

Shane pointed at Wrench. "You know Colin better than any of us. Dan trusted you and he was a good judge of character. It's your call."

Wrench retied the bandana around his head. He seemed to be in deep thought. Finally, he replied, "Colin wouldn't sell us out. Although, I probably wouldn't trust him with my wallet. I think it's like you said. He's probably been skimming the till. He may have headed off for greener pastures. He was never a fan of us getting involved in the shooting anyhow."

"Okay then." Shane glanced at his watch. "It's a quarter 'til eleven. The fireworks are scheduled to start in fifteen minutes."

Wrench waved at the bikers behind the boxcar. "Let's start moving into position."

Shane led the group up the railroad tracks which traced the Tuckasegee River to the hotel. "We'll head into those shrubs and wait until eleven o'clock on the nose to start shooting. We should have a good view of the troops who are outside of the building. Once we take them out, we'll go inside and clear it room by room."

When they arrived at the desired vantage point, Julianna pulled some branches of a shrub out of her way. "I don't see anyone outside."

"Maybe they found a new hangout after the Old Mill closed." Bobby stood high over the low bushes.

Shane considered the best course of action. "They could be in the lobby. We'll go in fast." He turned around. "Wrench, take three of your guys and secure the workers at the front desk. I don't want them catching a stray bullet, and I certainly don't want them calling up to the rooms to alert the others that the hotel is under attack. Try to get some key cards programmed to access all the rooms while you're at it. The manager should be able to do that for you."

"You got it," Wrench replied. "I'm sure we can convince him to cooperate."

"Okay, everyone move quickly and quietly." Shane left the cover of the shrubbery and sprinted toward the front entrance with the entire force trailing close behind him.

Once inside, Shane hurried past the front desk workers, paying them no mind and trusting Wrench to handle that area. Shane, Julianna, and Bobby rushed into the empty lobby. They scanned the immediate area and saw no one.

"What's going on?" Julianna looked around.

"I don't know." Shane led the way back to the front desk. "How's it coming with those key cards?"

"We're working on it." Wrench handed him three key cards with one hand while the other hand was on the shoulder of an extremely nervous shift manager.

The thin young man typed information on the keyboard frantically. "About five more minutes, sir."

Shane handed a card to two other team leaders among the Hill Runners. "You two, bring your teams upstairs with us. We'll work from the top floor down. My team will take low numbered rooms and work our way up. Your team will start from the high numbered rooms. Once the top floor is cleared, we'll take the stairs down to the next level and do the same."

Shane pointed at another team of Hill Runners. "You guys, watch the front door. The rest of you, come upstairs and find us when you get the key cards." To Wrench, he said, "Once you guys are done, zip tie the front desk workers then split into two teams and secure the stairwells."

"You bet," said Wrench.

Shane looked at all of them before he broke off.

"And remember, radio silence unless you need to warn another team of impending danger, or if you get in a pinch and need to be bailed out."

Shane, Julianna, Bobby, and the first team of Hill Runners squeezed into the elevator. The doors opened and Shane checked the hallway. "All clear. Let's go!" Shane stormed down the hall to the last room on the end.

Shane swiped the key card over the sensor for room 301. The light turned green and he pushed the handle. Bobby charged in ready to fire. Shane followed with Julianna behind him.

Julianna checked the bathroom. "All clear."

Dirty clothes were on the floor, the ashtray was full as was the garbage can, but no UN troops were inside. "Next room. Come on." Shane quickly led the way across the hall. He swiped the card over the sensor for room 302. Bobby pushed the door open just as he'd done for the previous room. Again, they found the room empty but with obvious signs of being lived in.

"They have to be somewhere." Shane led his team to 303, then 304. After coming out of 305, he paused to wait for a team of Hill Runners to emerge down the hall.

A burly biker came out of a room halfway down. He kept his rifle at a low-ready position and shrugged at Shane. Apparent by the lack of rifle fire, his team was coming up empty-handed as well. Shane signaled for the man to keep searching.

Shane kept his guard up as they entered room 306. He followed Bobby into yet another room with unmade beds and opened boxes of ammunition.

Suddenly, Shane's radio came to life.

"Shane, pick up! Let me know if you're alright!" It was the voice of Jimmy Teague with gunfire in the background. Evidently, his group had found no shortage of armed peacekeepers.

Shane pressed the talk key. "This is Shane, what's going on over there?"

Jimmy replied, "We're getting tore up. They've got at least 100 men at the sheriff's station, and another group of peacekeepers just rolled in behind us. They were ready for us. What's your situation?"

"This place is empty, I can't figure out what's going on, but we'll head in your direction to back you up."

"You better get here fast or there won't be anything left of us. We've lost ten shooters already, and I can't raise Johnny on the radio. I've been trying to call you for five minutes."

"These radios are line-of-sight. I'm on the top floor now, but probably too far from your location when I'm downstairs. Maybe Johnny is out of range also."

Jimmy continued, "We're completely pinned down. They've got armored vehicles all the way around our location. We don't have a chance of taking the building at this point. The best we can hope for is to slip out without all of us getting killed."

"What would be the best avenue of retreat for us to try to open up for you?"

"The north side is where they've been pushing us. We're trying to get up in those woods."

"We're on our way." Shane released the talk key

and pointed at the metal ammo cans. "Bobby, grab those. I think we're going to need them. Julianna and I will retrieve the ammo boxes from the other rooms." Shane called over the radio to the Hill Runners. "In case you folks downstairs didn't get that, Jimmy's team is getting ripped apart. Everyone, grab what ammo you can and meet downstairs. I don't think we're going to find any troops here."

Shane's team collected as much ammunition as they could carry and hustled down the stairs. When Shane reached the lobby, he waved to Wrench. "Back to the vehicles! We've got to move!"

Wrench sprinted out the door, hurrying to keep up with Shane. "I'm afraid we may have been sold out by Colin."

"Yeah, ya think?" Shane paced his breathing. "My only question is why the UN didn't have troops waiting for us at the hotel?"

Wrench grimaced as he dashed across the parking lot. "I'm guessing he told Abdulov about the action planned against the sheriff's department but didn't want to directly sell out the Hill Runners which would be assaulting the hotel."

Julianna kept pace with Shane and Wrench. "He had to have known that you'd respond to the ambush at the sheriff's department."

Wrench breathed heavily as he ran. "I'm sure he did, but you have to admit, we have a better chance of living through this than Johnny's people. Besides, it probably wouldn't have earned him a higher price for the information from Abdulov."

Bobby stayed close enough to the group to hear

the conversation. "Won't Abdulov want to kill Colin when he finds out he only got half the story?"

"Sure," said Wrench. "But Colin is long gone by now. No tellin' where, but if I had to guess, I'd say Black Hills."

"Sturgis?" Shane asked.

"Yep." Wrench slowed down when he reached the van he'd come in. "There's a few clubs holed up out there trying to survive."

Shane waved at the stragglers. "Hurry, everyone gather around me."

The gaggle of bikers panted, most of them in poor shape for such a long dash. They listened as Shane laid out the plan for striking the sheriff's department. "This is now an extraction operation. We'll get on the expressway and park on the shoulder of the road right before the Grindstaff exit. We'll work our way down into the trees between the expressway and the sheriff's department. From there, we'll try to draw the fire from the peacekeepers long enough for Jimmy's team to pull out. As soon as we've got all of them out of there, we have to get on the road before the UN can give chase. We can't fight them and win, so our only choice is to outrun them."

"Where are we going to go after?" asked one of the bikers.

"When I leave, follow me. I've got a place where we can all lay low for a few days." Shane got into the Ram and started the engine.

Shane punched the accelerator, kicking gravel and dust into the air as he sped out of the abandoned train yard. The expressway took a detour from the more direct route to the sheriff's department, but it was the only path which provided a means of escape from the overwhelming force of Abdulov's troops. "Is Wrench still behind us?"

Julianna turned to look behind them. "Wrench is. So are four other vehicles, but two of them just turned off."

Shane huffed. "Not worth the risk to them, I guess."

"There goes another one," Bobby added.

"So we're down to four total?" asked Shane.

"Wrench's van, and three pickups, it looks like," said Julianna.

Shane raced up the on-ramp and tore down US-74 toward the sheriff's department. He pulled to the shoulder and cut the engine just before reaching exit 83. "Let's go try to get Jimmy and Johnny out of there."

Shane hurdled over the guard rail and hustled down into the woods with Julianna and Bobby. The sound of gunfire was constant. Wrench and several other bikers who'd stuck with Shane followed close behind.

When Shane was close enough to distinguish friend from foe, he directed his shooters. "Wrench, take six of your guys down the exit ramp. You'll have a relatively unobstructed view from over there. Then wait for us to get into position. When you hear my team start shooting, join in and don't let up. If you can take out a hostile or two, that's fantastic, but our primary objective is to give Jimmy and Johnny enough cover fire to get out."

"Got it." Wrench pointed at the bikers he wanted

to follow him and headed toward the exit ramp.

Shane led his team and the remaining bikers further down the wooded hill. "That's Jimmy, trapped with Butterbean and those other five guys behind the black SUV. Bobby and Julianna, help me push back the peacekeepers on Jimmy's left flank. Hill Runners, you guys take the ones on the right." Shane took aim and began firing. He managed to kill two before the UN troops noticed his group was present, but they quickly found cover afterward.

Shane saw five or six other peacekeepers fall after being shot by members of Wrench's team. He watched as Jimmy assisted an injured man up the steep embankment. Shane soon recognized the wounded fighter as Jed, Johnny's son. Jed's leg was covered in blood. Next to him was his sister, Janie, who had her arm around his opposite side. Shane continued to cover them and many other members of the Jackson County group as they made their retreat.

Johnny's team managed to get up the hill. Shane paused from shooting long enough to lend a hand to Janie. "What are you doing out here?"

"I wanted to fight." Janie looked at Julianna. "Some of us aren't content to sit around and wait. Besides, you need every shooter you can get." She paused and looked past her uncle toward Butterbean and the stragglers still coming up the hill. "Have you seen my dad?"

"I'm afraid not." Shane let out another volley of cover fire toward the peacekeepers.

Jimmy sounded winded. "Janie, I need you to help me get Jed to the trucks. He's bleeding bad."

She turned and examined her brother's leg. "I'm not leaving without dad."

Shane replied, "You might have to. The peacekeepers aren't that far behind the stragglers. If we miss our opportunity to get out of here, we'll all be dead."

Her face contorted in sorrow. "I can't. I can't leave Dad!"

Julianna changed magazines and placed a gentle hand on Janie's shoulder. "Focus on helping your brother for now."

Janie hesitated before putting her arm around her brother to assist Jimmy in getting him to the vehicles.

Shane assumed the worst had happened to Johnny. "Butterbean, you have to move it!"

The heavy man nodded and huffed as he continued steadily up the hill.

Shane watched three more of the Jackson County group get gunned down while attempting to withdraw from the action. "I don't see Johnny. We need to get out of here. Abdulov will have his MRAPs up here on the highway soon and we'll have no chance of a getaway."

Butterbean was the last man up the hill. He fell to his knees and panted for air upon arrival.

Bobby called out to the bikers shooting from the exit ramp. "Wrench! Come on! We're moving out!"

Shane's team kept up the pressure with their rifles until the Hill Runners were back to the vehicles. "That's the last of them. Let's go!" He patted Julianna and Bobby on their backs and waited for them to start toward the truck before

ceasing to fire. He pulled Butterbean up and pushed
him toward the escape vehicles.

CHAPTER 19

And call upon me in the day of trouble: I will deliver thee, and thou shalt glorify me. But unto the wicked God saith, What hast thou to do to declare my statutes, or that thou shouldest take my covenant in thy mouth? Seeing thou hatest instruction, and casteth my words behind thee.

Psalm 50:15-17

Shane sped down the highway. He glanced back to see Jimmy and Janie in the bed of the truck caring for Jed's injured leg. Several other fighters from Jackson County were also crammed into the small space in the rear of the vehicle. "Does anyone see UN vehicles behind us?"

"Nothing yet." Julianna studied the side view

mirror from the passenger's seat. "All of the Hill Runners are staying close to us."

"Good, because I can't slow down." Shane pressed the accelerator. "Did anyone get a count of how many of our people made it out of that mess?"

Butterbean sat in the backseat with Bobby. "I counted thirty, including the injured."

"Sixty went in with you?" Julianna turned to face Butterbean.

"Yeah, that's about right," he replied.

"At least ten of the Hill Runners jumped ship," said Shane. "That means we've got less than fifty shooters left. I realize those are friends, family members, and neighbors who we lost back there, but the sentiment doesn't change the math."

"We can't take on Abdulov's forces now," said Bobby.

Julianna hardened her jaw. "We can't give up either."

"We'll figure it out when we get to camp. For now, let's just focus on treating our wounded and staying alive through the night." Shane had enough on his plate without worrying about what they'd do tomorrow.

***

The next morning, Julianna shook Shane's arm. She'd slept next to him in the loft of Paw Paw's old distillery barn. She whispered so not to wake any of the other militia members who were also using the structure as a refuge. "Shane, wake up. It's Sunday. You need to say something today— to encourage people."

"You mean like church? I can't imagine anyone is in the mood for church." He rolled back over. "Least of all, me."

"Which is exactly why you need to say something. You can't let this spirit of defeat linger. You have to put together a message. It doesn't need to be long, but the whole camp is counting on you to tell them everything is going to be okay and that God is still in control."

"How am I going to sell that when I don't even believe it?"

"You don't think God is still on His throne?"

"Yes, but I'm not so sure He's going to deliver us out of this one."

"Then just tell them God is still in charge, that He's still sovereign. They need something to believe in—even if you don't."

Her pointed comment spurred him from his less-than-comfortable position inside the thin sleeping bag rolled out on the uneven wooden planks of the loft. "Okay. I'll get my Bible out of my pack. I'll have something together by 10:00."

"We should sing a couple of songs also."

"I didn't bring my guitar."

"Cole brought it. It's inside the shotgun house with him and Angela."

"Okay then. I guess we'll do church." Shane slipped his feet inside his boots and climbed down from the loft. He retrieved his Bible from the truck. He found a quiet place by the creek and sat down. He turned to the Psalms to find an encouraging word, both for the others at the camp and for himself.

"God help me. I make mistakes. I'm unprepared and unequipped as a pastor. I suppose the same could be said about my role as a soldier and a leader."

Shane lifted his head. He recalled a statement from his younger years, one he'd heard Pastor Joel say many times. *God doesn't call the qualified. He qualifies the called.*

***

Later that afternoon, at a clearing near the creek, Shane finished off his MRE, giving half of his chocolate bar to Cole. Jimmy came to sit next to them. "That was a good message you gave this morning."

"Thanks. I wish I could have said more to comfort Jed, Janie, and Johnny's wife." Shane put his arm around his son.

"I don't think anyone can comfort them." Sitting directly on the ground, Jimmy crossed his legs and leaned back on his hands. "It's one thing when you have a body to say goodbye to. It's quite another when the person is just gone."

"How are you holding up?" Shane asked. "The two of you were close."

"Yep." Jimmy looked up at the treetops which were becoming increasingly bare with the fading of autumn. "We had a lot of good memories growing up together, running the hills of North Carolina as boys—without a care in the world. I'm going to miss him. But I've got Mandy and the kids. It's different for his wife, Janie, and Jed. For them, Dad's gone."

"Mrs. Betty seems to be taking it rough." Shane stroked Cole's jet-black hair.

Jimmy looked at the babbling brook. "Parents never expect to outlive their children. It doesn't feel right when they do. Pop is having a hard time with it also. The important thing is for his death to not be in vain."

Shane pulled Cole close. He could sense the direction in which the conversation was going.

Jimmy looked over at him. "We need to ask Caleb Creech for help."

Shane shook his head. "He's not going to upset the apple cart for some little town 300 miles away. We're customers to Creech—nothing more."

"Then let's be customers," said Jimmy. "Who says gas and diesel are the only markets he wants to be involved with?"

"You're suggesting he should enter the mercenary business?" Shane pressed his lips together in anticipation of Jimmy's response.

"I'm saying he might already be participating in it. He's got guns, vehicles, men, heavy weapons; do you think Creech is the type to let assets like that sit idle?"

"They're not idle," Shane rebutted. "His small private military is providing him with the leverage he needs to maintain his position with the ESC."

"But he could utilize his army to generate a profit instead of it being merely an overhead expense."

Shane sighed. "Even if his little militia was for

hire, what do you suggest we offer to pay them with?"

Jimmy looked Shane in the eyes. He paused before speaking. "I have no right to ask this of you. And you owe us nothing. But we can't survive out here at this compound indefinitely. We don't have the supplies or the resources for this many people. That won't even be an issue if Abdulov decides to hunt us down. And I'm not asking because I want vengeance for my brother's death, although I'm sure my parents, along with Johnny's wife and kids, would like to see justice served…"

"Go on," said Shane. "Get to the point."

Jimmy looked at the ground, then back up to Shane's eyes. "If you have the means to make an offer, we'd all be indebted to you—for life."

Shane looked around at the fallen leaves covering the sloping piece of ground leading down toward the rushing creek. "I have a few gold coins from my father. Maybe about fifty or so. But they belong to Angela also. She'd have to be on board with it. I also have the ring I bought for Lilith, but I'm not sure it would be enough to get Creech to move against the ESC."

"All he can do is say no," said Jimmy.

"No, he could turn me in to them, if he thought he could make a profit out of the deal. Money has no sides. We learned that the hard way with Colin."

Jimmy picked up a twig and toyed with it between his fingers. "Creech doesn't strike me as the same type of character as Colin. Colin was a bottom feeder when we met him. Unfortunately, he was the best person for the job at the time. We didn't have an extensive list of candidates for the position of seedy, black-market biker."

"I'll talk to Angela. If she'll sign off on using her share of the coins, I'll go see Creech. But I can't make any promises about what he'll say."

"That's all I'm asking for." Jimmy stood up and brushed the leaves off of the back of his pants. "Thank you, Shane. We all need this one. Otherwise, we don't stand a chance at getting our homes back."

Shane nodded. "I just hope we don't end up making matters worse."

***

Monday morning, Shane, Bobby, and Julianna loaded into the Ram.

"Mind if I come along for the ride?" Wrench carried a duffle bag over his shoulder. "I get antsy when I don't have my bikes and tools to keep me busy."

"Suit yourself," said Shane. "But I'll warn you, it's a long ride, and it's been known to be dangerous in the past."

"I don't mind the ride." Wrench tossed his bag into the bed of the truck. "I can't imagine we'd have much trouble. The UN has things fairly well locked down."

"I don't know." Julianna opened the passenger side door and placed her rifle inside. "Renegade bikers and insurgency groups are known to be operating in these parts."

"Is she talking about us?" Wrench got into the

back seat with Bobby.

"She might be talking about you, but I'm an upstanding member of society." Bobby grinned.

Shane started the engine. "All jokes aside, running into a patrol of peacekeepers is our most likely threat. If they pull us over. Wait until they get to the side of the vehicle, then start shooting. No doubt they're looking for us. We won't be able to talk our way out of it if we're stopped."

The drive to Catlettsburg was uneventful. However, the same could not be said for Shane's arrival at Caleb Creech's refinery.

"Out of the vehicle! Hands up where we can see them!" A guard with a black facemask pointed an AK-47 at the Ram.

"I thought you said you were on good terms with these guys," said Wrench.

Shane held his hands up and slowly opened his door. "We usually come in a tanker truck."

"On the ground!" Another black-clad guard jerked Shane from the vehicle and forced him to the ground.

"We're friends with Caleb Creech!" Shane looked under the truck to see another guard with his knee on Julianna's back.

"What's your name?" asked the guard holding Shane down.

"Shane Black."

The guard called out to another one of the men on the security team, "Call Creech. Ask him if he knows a Shane Black."

Shane waited for the reply to come over the radio.

"Let them in," yelled another guard. "Creech said to give them back their weapons."

The guard helped Shane up off the ground but did not apologize for the rough treatment. "Get back in the vehicle and drive through."

Shane didn't mention the lack of courtesy, but neither did he thank the man for granting him access. Once inside the truck, Shane looked at the passengers one by one. "Everybody okay?"

"My pride is a little scraped up," Bobby joked.

Shane pulled through the steel gate into the refinery compound. "I bet you're wishing you'd have stayed home, Wrench."

"I wasn't expecting a guided tour of the facility with complimentary ice cream, but I wasn't anticipating a TSA pat-down either," the biker replied.

Shane parked at the administrative building. Creech's personal bodyguard, Mickey, met Shane and his team at the door. "Follow me, please."

Mickey was a man of few words, which suited Shane just fine. Shane and the others followed him up the stairs to Creech's office. Mickey held the door open for them when they arrived.

"Shane Black. Come on in here." Creech broke into a coughing fit. His mechanical hand abandoned the cigar he'd been smoking in the ashtray on his desk. Creech picked up a glass with his good hand and took a drink. Whatever the substance in the glass was, it appeared to ease his coughing.

"Have a seat, please." Creech motioned to the couch and chairs in the rear of the sprawling executive suite. Julianna, Bobby, and Wrench all found a place to sit down.

Shane, however, sat in the single wooden chair in front of Creech's large mahogany desk.

"I understand the boys were a little rough when you arrived. I apologize for that, but I had no idea you were coming. They know to treat customers better than that, but we don't get many people showing up in pickup trucks these days."

"We survived," said Shane.

"Did something happen to your tanker truck?" Creech asked.

"No," said Shane. "We didn't come for gas."

"Oh?" Creech listened closely as Shane told him of the trouble Jackson County was having with the ESC.

By the end of the tale, Creech seemed to have forgotten his adversity to cigars as he took out his brass Zippo to light another one. He puffed it a few times to get the ember glowing red hot, then blew a long puff of smoke up toward the ceiling. "I hear the fire is still burning in the park. That's a very unfortunate turn of events. I wouldn't exactly describe my relationship with the UN as mutually-beneficial, but we're both trying to make the best of it.

"I hate to sound like an armchair quarterback, but it sounds to me like you had a more advantageous association with this Abdulov fellow when you were selling him liquor. I believe I'd have tried to parlay that into a better working alliance."

"We didn't get into the liquor business for the sake of making a profit and getting in good with the ESC. We had a set objective. It was part of a larger plan."

Creech dusted the ashes off of his cigar with the pair of metal hooks on his prosthetic. "You tried and you lost. I empathize with your position, but I really don't see how I can help you, Shane."

"You could let us hire some of your soldiers so we can take back our town."

Creech started laughing, which soon morphed into yet another coughing fit. He pointed his mechanical hooks at Shane. "Then where would that leave me? I have to keep up a show of force. If the ESC sees that I'm weak, they could very quickly decide to take over the facility."

"They know you're well-armed and well-staffed. They'd never notice a few men gone for a day or two."

"Not that I'd even consider doing such a crazy thing, but how many is a few?" Creech puffed the cigar.

"A hundred," said Shane.

"A hundred? You *must* think I'm crazy. Even with my reserve men over in Huntington, that would leave me with fifty men to cover all three shifts. I guarantee the UN would notice."

"Eighty," Shane countered.

Creech shook his head. "No, no, no. Shane, we're not negotiating."

"You told me that you're always negotiating."

"Well, not this time. I'm showing you the courtesy of hearing you out, but I'm afraid I can't help you."

From his pocket, Shane pulled out two plastic tubes of one-ounce gold coins. He placed them on

Creech's desk. "There's forty ounces of gold for eighty men. We can eliminate every one of the peacekeepers holed up in Jackson County."

Creech let his smoldering cigar rest in the ashtray. He held one of the tubes with his prosthetic and pulled the cap off with his good hand. Creech poured a couple of the coins into his hand and examined them.

Shane continued to build his case. "You've got a bunch of junkyard dogs out there. They must be getting restless guarding a gate all day and all night. Some action would probably do them good.'

Creech didn't argue but continued looking at the coins. "Even so, I couldn't be eighty men short. The ESC Resource Administrator would catch wind of it. He'd know my men were involved in your little rebellion."

"Sixty," said Shane.

Creech stood up from his desk. "You're asking me to bite the hand that feeds me."

"We both know that's not an accurate description of your relationship with the ESC. In fact, this will make you more valuable to them."

"How so?" Creech looked out his window toward the autumn painted mountains in the distance.

"For every little enclave like Jackson County that fails, the more Maris Allard needs to be able to taunt another success story like the famous renaissance city of Huntington, West Virginia. The ESC knows you could burn this refinery down, pull your support for the UN, and incite an insurrection.

"Huntington might be the straw that breaks the

241

camel's back. The fall of Jackson County will serve as a reminder of just how important Caleb Creech is to the Economic Stability Commission."

The grizzled old man picked up his cigar with his mechanical hand and took a puff. He dusted off the ashes and pointed the glowing ember at Shane. "You should have been a union negotiator." He smiled revealing tobacco-stained teeth. "Forty ounces, I could do forty men. Armed and ready for battle."

"An ounce of gold for each man?"

"I'm going to have to give them hazard pay. Plus I'm risking being short-staffed here while they're gone. They'll expend ammunition. Some of them probably won't make it back. This ain't a rental car." Creech removed the coins from the tubes to count and inspect each one. "And you knew I wasn't runnin' no charity when you came up here. I like you as much as I like anyone, but this is a business."

Shane considered the possibility. The last thing he wanted to do was to lead another failed raid against Abdulov. He pulled another ten ounces out of his pocket. He removed them from the plastic tube and put them on the desk. "Make it fifty men and let me borrow your tank."

"My tank?" Creech's bushy brows raised high on his wrinkled forehead. "You've got a better chance of me lending you my refinery! As soon as the Resource Administrator hears there was a tank involved, he'll know exactly where it came from."

"Then he'll know that it's not just for looks," Shane countered. "Besides, we don't plan on leaving any talebearers."

"Yeah, easier said than done."

"We need it. Abdulov is using the sheriff's department as his base of operations. We have to punch some holes in the walls if we have any hope of taking it. Otherwise, it's another suicide mission."

"What about some RPGs?" Creech looked at the stack of coins on the desk.

"We have to have the tank. The UN has armored vehicles."

"I can get you armored vehicles. I'll even throw in a couple for nothing. I'll consider it insurance for getting my men back home alive."

"Thanks, but I really need to use your tank. We need to overwhelm them. I can't do this if it's not certain that we'll get our town back."

"There's no guarantee of that anyway. Even if you have a favorable outcome, the ESC could roll in with twice as many UN troops the next day."

"They won't," said Shane. "Not with the forest burning and no way to offset the expenditure. Otherwise, they would have fought harder to hold the big cities. Jackson County isn't worth the effort."

Creech sat back down. He pushed the pile of coins toward Shane. "I'd love to help you, but you're not getting my tank."

Shane reached in his pocket. He pulled out the diamond ring he'd bought for Lilith. Shane placed the monster 3-carat stone on top of the pile of gold coins. "I'm not asking you to do it out of the kindness of your heart."

Creech stared at the giant sparkling rock for a moment. He retrieved a loupe out of his desk and picked up the ring to inspect it. How much did this one set you back?"

"Over a hundred grand," said Shane. "That was back when a hundred thousand dollars was worth something."

"Those were the days." Creech seemed mesmerized by the dazzling object on the opposite side of his jeweler's loupe.

After giving him an adequate amount of time for admiration, Shane asked, "So, do we have a deal?"

"When are you planning to embark on your little escapade?" Creech did not look up.

"Wednesday night, provided we have the necessary soldiers and weapons."

Creech opened the drawer of his desk. He placed the diamond and the loupe inside. "You're gonna owe me for this."

"What do you mean?"

"If I ever ask a favor of you, you'll be obliged to grant it. You can't turn me down."

"Sounds like a mob deal."

"What you're asking for is typically the kind of thing you'd go to a criminal enterprise for."

"Let's be clear about what types of favors you might ask of me."

"Well, I ain't gonna have you come up here and wax my Cadillac. If I call on you, it will be to fight. I'm in good with the current resource administrator, Marty Schnagel, but he could get promoted, he could mess around and get himself killed, or he might just get greedy. The ESC could bring in some other squirrelly little fella to take his place. The next one may or may not honor the agreement I have with Schnagel."

"So, I'm hiring out your militia at top dollar, but if you ever get in a pinch, I'd be expected to drop everything and come fight for you pro bono? I'll admit you have me over a barrel on this one, Mr. Creech, but that's asking too much." Shane began raking the coins off the desk to put back in the plastic tubes.

Creech reached across the desk to grab Shane's hand. "Hold on, now. Nobody ever said anything about you having to work for free. I'd compensate you. Plus you'd have your share of the spoils. Which reminds me, my men will be taking back half of whatever you recover from the operation in Sylva."

Shane eyed the old union boss. "Compensated how?"

"We'll figure that out when and if the need arises."

"I'm committing to a contract here. We'll state the terms clearly right now. If myself or anyone from Sylva is to be conscripted into service with you, we want the same pay your men are getting. We want one ounce of gold each. And I want it in writing. Otherwise, you can take that diamond back out of your desk and give it to me right now." Shane's brows sank deep into his forehead.

Caleb Creech grinned. With his mechanical claw, he retrieved a pen from a collection of writing instruments stashed in a USW coffee mug. With his good hand, he pulled out a yellow legal pad from the bottom drawer of his desk. "I taught you to be too good of a negotiator."

Shane watched the man begin to enumerate the terms of the agreement. "We also need to agree on how many shooters would be obliged to participate if such an instance were to occur."

"I'd like to have the option to hire fifty."

"We don't have fifty shooters now." Shane looked back at Wrench. "The Hill Runners who are with us live in the next town up. They're working with us as a favor. Like I said, we took heavy losses when we tried to take the sheriff's department the first time."

"You should have come to see me before you jumped into that briar patch." Creech continued writing.

"We thought we could handle it. We would have pulled it off if we hadn't been sold down the river by one of our own."

Creech paused. "Twenty-five, then. I need at least that many to make it worth my while."

Shane nodded. "Fine."

"And since we're negotiating for a smaller number of soldiers than what I'm supplying you with, the terms are one ounce of gold or the equivalent value in gas, diesel, or silver."

Shane looked back to Julianna before answering.

She lifted her shoulders. "That's the difference between getting paid in hundreds or twenties as far as I can tell."

Shane looked back to Creech. "Okay, but if you pay us in fuel, you have to deliver it to Sylva."

"Don't take advantage of my generosity." Creech

stitched his brows together.

"Yeah, right." Shane laughed. "There's little threat of that."

Creech handed the paper to Shane to look over. "Does this appear to be agreeable?"

Shane examined the hand-written contract. "I think that covers it." Shane signed on his line and gave it back to Creech.

"Very well." Creech signed the bottom of the paper and made a copy of it. He handed the copy to Shane. "Give directions to Mickey. I'll make sure your men and the tank are at that location by noon on Wednesday."

Shane folded the paper and stuck it in his pocket. "All the hardnose horse-trading aside, I appreciate this, Mr. Creech. It means a lot to us." Shane offered his hand to the man.

Creech stood up to shake with Shane. "I'm glad I can help. I like you, Shane Black. I always have."

CHAPTER 20

The horse is prepared against the day of battle: but safety is of the Lord.

Proverbs 21:31

Late Wednesday morning, Shane's radio sprang to life. "We've got company. Lots of it."

Shane stood up on the small porch of the shotgun house at the Ensley's fallback compound in Murphy. He checked his watch then pressed the talk key. "It should be our auxiliary force coming down from Kentucky, but everyone look alive. Let's stay ready for anything until we've confirmed they're friendlies."

Shane knocked on the door. "Bobby, Julianna, y'all come on out here."

Bobby was first through the door. He flipped the

safety off of his AK-47. "Maybe we should give them the same kind of welcome they gave us."

Julianna was next. She held her AR ready to fire and hustled down the steps. "I'm so glad that they showed up, I'm thinking of baking them a pie."

"Let's save the punishments and rewards until we know that it's actually them." Shane rushed ahead to take the lead.

The first vehicle drove up the long dirt road to where Shane waited. The heavy-duty pickup truck rolled to a stop. Four men were in the cab and six more in the bed of the truck. All were armed and appeared ready for battle.

Shane looked past the driver to the man in the passenger's seat. "Mickey?"

Mickey waved at Shane. "Mr. Creech wanted me to personally ensure that all the men act in accordance with his standards of professionalism and that you're completely satisfied with their work."

Shane smiled. "Thank you. I appreciate you coming along."

"Okay, if you don't mind, we'll get everyone unloaded so we can go over the plan of attack."

"Sure. You can park in that clearing past the large oak." Shane pointed in the direction they should go. He watched as the additional vehicles drove past. The third was a semi-truck hauling a flatbed trailer. The payload was covered with a large beige tarp. Shane hoped it was the tank but the shape of the item had been obscured by large frames beneath the tarp.

Shane followed the heavy delivery until the

driver parked. Mickey walked over to his side. Without saying anything, he began untying the tarp. Shane assisted him and took a peek underneath when an adequate number of ties had been removed.

"Is that what you were hoping to find?" Mikey asked.

"That will do it." Shane admired the gargantuan war implement. "Did you bring a crew to operate it?"

Mickey pointed at the semi driver. "Davis is the driver. Keith and Ronald are the gunners. Mr. Creech included ten 120mm shells. Technically, they're obstacle reduction rounds, but it usually doesn't go well for anyone on the other side of the obstacle being reduced."

"Okay. Let's head to the barn. We'll go over our basic strategy." Shane led Mickey and the rest of the men toward the planning area inside the distillery.

"Smells like sour mash," Mickey commented as they walked the short path through the woods.

Julianna answered, "This place used to be a distillery back during prohibition."

"Smells like it's been active a little more recently than that," said Mickey.

"We had it in operation for a short time. We were trading booze for guns." Shane led the group out into the clearing where the barn stood.

"You should keep it going. Big money in liquor," said Mickey.

"It doesn't reflect our values." Shane opened the door and led the group inside.

"It's a shame to let it go to waste." Mickey eyed the large copper kettles.

Shane took them to a large cleared space where several sections of cut logs served as makeshift stools for them to sit upon. "Everyone find a seat. I'll go over the basic plan using the map on the blackboard. After I'm finished, we'll open up the floor to questions. Ten shooters will take up sniper positions by the hotel which the peacekeepers are using as a barracks. The rest of us will attack their base of operations, the old sheriff's department. Once we've eliminated all hostiles at the sheriff's department, we'll go to the hotel and clear it room by room."

"Quick question before you get started," Mickey said.

"Sure."

"Do you have any opposition to destroying the hotel and the sheriff's department? Ten rounds should be enough to raze both."

"I don't have any problem with that at all," said Shane. "If we get our town back, we'll find another building for a sheriff's department."

"Good to know." Mickey gestured with his hand to the audience of fighters waiting for Shane's instructions. "Please continue."

***

Wednesday night, Shane turned off his lights and pulled to the side of the road about a quarter-mile up the expressway from the Jackson County Sheriff's Department.

Julianna got out of the vehicle and closed the door quietly. "You'd think they would have put a guard on this road, considering this is the direction we attacked them from last time."

"I hope they aren't expecting us at all." Shane got out and waved at the driver of the next vehicle to park behind him. "They sent us packing with heavy losses last time. They probably think we'd have to be insane to come back for more."

Butterbean held his rifle close to his chest. "They might be right about that."

"Too late to debate whether or not it's the sane thing to do." Bobby watched the semi-truck arrive near the end of the line.

"We're here now." Shane stepped out into the road and signaled for the driver to bring the tank to the front of the line.

Mickey approached Shane. "We're split up into two platoons like you asked."

"Good." Shane pointed down the embankment. "These are the woods which your people will be using for cover. Platoon Alpha will be on this side and Bravo will be right next to them. Both will be attacking from the west."

The tank operator and gunner team arrived next. Shane continued talking. "We'll circle around with the tank. Once we get about halfway down the exit ramp, we'll have a clear shot at the building from the north side. Gunners, hit the north wall about four times. Then take the tank down into the parking lot. Once we see where the activity is inside, we'll advise where to place the next couple of rounds. I'd like to save at least three shells to take the hotel, but this building is our priority. Radio silence until the action starts."

"We can handle that," said the tank operator.

"Good." Shane checked his watch. "Then let's take 'em out."

Shane led his team along with the Hill Runners toward the exit ramp. Once in position, he waited for the tank to get in place.

Julianna lay prone next to Shane beneath the cover of the trees, which acted as a border between the exit ramp and the parking lot of the sheriff's station. "I've never heard a tank fire. Is it loud?"

Bobby went down to one knee behind the trunk of the tree. "I would imagine so."

"We should have brought ear protection," Butterbean said.

"If we live through this, I'll learn sign language." Shane looked at the building through the scope of his rifle.

"Yeah, me, too," Julianna replied. "But it would help if we could hear our radios during this operation."

Shane grimaced. He'd not considered that threat and had no idea what to expect when the big 120mm gun erupted. Shane watched the turret swing toward the sheriff's department. He stuck his fingers in his ears hoping it would help.

Booom!!! The ground shook beneath his body. BOOWWM! Then, the impact blast of the exploding shell rocked the earth even more. Shane kept his fingers in his ears as he watched the turret adjust. The big gun fired once more.

Shane looked over to see Bobby's lips moving.

He took his fingers out of his ears. "What did you say?"

Bobby spoke loudly, "I said, they have to know that they are under attack by now."

"Yeah, I'd say you're right about that."

Julianna nudged Shane and pointed at the tank. "He's getting ready to fire again!"

Shane placed his fingers back in his ears just in time to buffer the deafening report. The tank began to crawl forward over the mound, separating the exit ramp from the sheriff's department parking lot. The rolling fortress paused to fire once more before continuing its steady march into the parking lot.

"They're coming out!" Wrench pointed at UN troops running from the building.

"They're trying to get to the armored vehicles!" Shane shouted. "We have to stop them." He led the charge behind the tank, down the embankment, and into the parking lot. Shane stayed near the tank for cover and took a shot each time he saw a peacekeeper emerge from the building, which was crumbling on both sides and in the middle.

He pressed the talk key of his radio. "Mickey, I need you to bring Alpha and Bravo in. We have to keep the enemy away from those armored vehicles."

"Roger. We're on it," Mickey replied.

"Shane, this is the tank gunner. You've got three armored vehicles on the south end of the parking lot. I could probably take out all three of them with one shot the way they're lined up right now."

Shane fired three more rounds at UN troops coming out the gaping hole on the south side of the building. He paused to press the mic key on his radio. "I like the way you think, but let's hold off until we see peacekeepers get inside. If possible, I want to keep those vehicles as spoil, not to mention we're trying to conserve tank ammunition. But keep your eye on them. If you see even one soldier make it to a vehicle, light 'em all up."

"Roger that," said the gunner.

Shane led Julianna, Bobby, Butterbean, Wrench and a collection of other fighters from Jackson County and the Hill Runners toward the row of armored vehicles. "Come on. Let's try to take cover behind those UN trucks. We can use them as a fighting position and keep the peacekeepers away."

No sooner had Shane led his squad out from behind the tank than the echo of .50 caliber rounds rang out from above. Shane looked back to make sure Julianna was close behind him. "Run!"

She kept pace with Shane. Bobby and Wrench stayed close behind. Butterbean struggled to keep up. Shane dropped to the ground once he made it behind the nearest UN truck. He looked under the vehicle and between the tires to see three people from his squad fall. Shane quickly addressed the tank. "Gunner, I need you to eliminate the big machine gun on the roof."

"I'm already on it," came the reply.

Shane heard the giant gun blast. He looked out from behind the truck at the roofline of the sheriff's department to see a hollow crater where the .50 cal machine gun had been. "Wrench, Bobby, grab three more guys. We've got to go get our people out of the parking lot. Julianna, you're in charge of everyone else. We need cover fire while we're out there."

"Hurry!" She took aim and began peppering the building with rifle fire while Shane and the others left the cover of the vehicles.

Shane stopped at the first casualty. The man was someone from Sylva. He'd been shot in the hip and appeared to be in great pain. "Look at me! We're going to get you home!"

The man winced in agony but managed to nod as Shane lifted him up from the ground. One of the bikers assisted Shane in getting the man up from the pavement and back to safety. When they arrived back to the vehicles, Shane called on his radio, "I need medics to the three white armored vehicles on the south side."

"We're on our way," came a reply.

Mickey's voice was next over the radio. "You've got them all stressed out inside there. You need to seize upon the confusion—before they can calm down and start thinking rationally about how to get out of the mess they're in."

"Okay," Shane replied. "Let's get inside and start mopping up. Have Bravo set up a perimeter to take out anyone who tries to flee. Then, bring Alpha down here to the south side. We'll make entry together."

"Be there in two," said Mickey.

Shane put his hand on Julianna's shoulder. "You stay here with Butterbean and the bikers. Provide cover for us in case we have to pull out and protect the armored vehicles."

She slapped a fresh magazine in the bottom of her rifle. "Yeah, right." She positioned herself to participate in the assault against the building.

Bobby lined up behind Shane. He patted him on the back. "You gave it your best shot."

Shane frowned. "Wrench, can you keep eight of your guys back here to guard the vehicles?"

"You don't have to ask me twice." Wrench seemed grateful to not be going inside the demolished structure.

"Thanks." Shane watched Mickey lead his men to the rally point from the trees. Once they were all present, Shane called out, "We'll enter through the blast hole on the south side and work our way north. Once we clear the first floor, we'll work on the second."

"We'll follow you." Mickey motioned for his men to get ready.

"Okay, let's go!" Shane sprinted toward the building. He slowed down before entering. "This place is a mess!" He stepped over piles of crumbled concrete. Shane scanned the inside of the building for hostiles. He saw none but dispatched three injured troops scattered about the floor.

"They didn't look like they were going to make it anyway." Julianna kept her rifle ready to fire. "It's unrecognizable as the sheriff's department."

A dangling fluorescent light fixture dropped from the ceiling and crashed on a soot-covered desk. Bobby proceeded cautiously. "Yeah, it's been extensively remodeled."

Shane stepped over several dead bodies. POP, POP, POP! A surge of automatic gunfire ripped through the damaged drywall. "Get down!" Shane grabbed Julianna and pulled her to the ground.

"Cover us!" Mickey signaled for eight men to follow him. "We'll flank 'em."

Shane shouldered his rifle and fired blindly into the wall from where the gunfire had originated.

Mickey led his team into the next room and opened up a barrage of heavy fire. Their weapons grew silent. "All clear."

Shane waved for his team to follow and they continued the search. When they came to the main reception area, the floor was littered with peacekeepers. Shane inspected the faces of them, searching for anyone he might recognize. "Keep an eye out for Abdulov."

Julianna put her hand on Shane's arm and turned him around. "This guy lost his head from the tank round."

Shane's stomach knotted at the gruesome sight. "That's not a UN uniform."

"No. He was a civilian," Julianna said.

Bobby flipped the headless corpse over and read the title on his shirt, "Deputy Constable."

Shane examined the corpse's hands. Sure enough, one of them was missing a pinky. The scar was healed. The injury was not from the same trauma which had liberated the corpse of its head. "It's Greg."

"That's convenient for you." Julianna glanced back at Bobby.

Bobby made no comment.

Shane looked at his old friend, then back to Julianna. "What's that supposed to mean?"

"Are you serious? You don't know?" Julianna adjusted her rifle.

"Know what?" Shane looked at Bobby.

"I've been meaning to talk to you about something," said the big man. "But it never seemed like the right time."

"Angela?" Shane was completely caught off guard.

"Now is not the right time either." Julianna turned Shane around and nudged him forward. "Let's survive this and then we can all have a nice long chat."

In the next room, the team encountered another group of UN troops, many of whom were injured from the tank blast but were still quite capable of firing their weapons. Shane found cover behind a cement pillar and began shooting. Volleys of ammunition flew in both directions for several minutes. Shane picked off two peacekeepers and the rest of his teammates killed many others, but the attack persisted.

Bobby yelped in pain. "Ahhh!"

Shane's heart jumped. "Bobby!" He hurdled over a metal beam which had dropped from the gaping hole in the ceiling to get to his friend.

Bobby pointed up. "Shooters on the second floor."

Shane examined the wound in Bobby's leg. He was bleeding badly. "Help!" He waved for some of the other fighters from Sylva to assist him in getting Bobby out of range of the second-floor troops.

Three of them rushed to his aid. It took the strength of them all to move the big fellow. Shane quickly placed a tourniquet over the wound. "Stay here until we can get this place cleaned out. Then

I'll come back to get you."

"I'm not going anywhere." Bobby was in deep distress but could still fire his rifle if need be.

Once the remaining hostiles on the ground level were killed, Shane led the assault through the rest of the building to the north side. Shane looked up at the stairwell which had been hit by a tank round. "We can't get upstairs this way."

Mickey looked at the missing section of stairs. "A couple of us could hold our hands and hoist the others up to the rail. They can pull themselves up and onto the landing."

Shane looked at the mishmash of fighters under his command. Many were far too out of shape to be pulling themselves up onto the landing. "Raise your hand if you are certain you can do a pull-up."

Less than a third of them put their hand in the air. Shane nodded. "Okay, those of you who can't, put your hands together and interlace your fingers to form steps for the rest of us to climb up on."

Shane led the way. He put his foot into the first man's hand and pushed himself up to grab the rail. Shane struggled but managed to get himself up and over. Next was Julianna. He grabbed her arm and helped her onto the landing. The two of them assisted Mickey in getting across the missing steps, then the others came. Shane looked down at the group who had no chance of getting up to the second floor. "The rest of you, split up and cover the openings to the second floor. As we make our way through the building, we'll have plenty of troops try to drop down and make a run for it."

Shane led his team to begin clearing the upper

floor. Immediately, they encountered more gunfire.

"Grenade!" Mickey jumped back behind the wall.

Shane watched the heavy metal object bounce right at his feet. Time froze. He knew he could not escape the blast and doubted his body would offer enough of a shield to protect Julianna. In an instant, he picked it up and hurled it back through the doorway it had come out of. As soon as the pineapple-shaped instrument of destruction had left his hand, he tackled Julianna to the ground.

BOOM!

Shane felt the blast but couldn't be sure if any of the shrapnel had hit him. He rolled over and did a quick inspection.

Mickey helped him up. "Lucky for you, they didn't cook that thing off before they tossed it. That was some fast action on your part."

Shane looked heavenward. "Thank you, God!"

Julianna pulled him back as the next wave of gunfire erupted from the next room. "Nice work, but you didn't get them all."

Shane shot into the room. He paused to look at some of his men. "Cover me. I need to get close to the door so I can shoot inside the next room."

Mickey put his hand on his shoulder. "I'm with you."

"Me, too," said Julianna.

The rest of the team fired through the door while Shane crawled to the opening. He fired inside in a typical spray-and-pray fashion. Mickey did the same from the opposite side of the door.

A voice shouted from inside. "Hold the room!

Don't let them in!"

"That's Abdulov!" Julianna said from behind Shane.

"We need to breach," said Mickey.

Shane nodded. "Will you stay out here?" he asked Julianna.

"Not on your life," she replied.

"Then at least stay behind me," he insisted.

Mickey motioned for the other fighters to stack up behind himself and Shane. "On three." He held up his hand and counted off the numbers with his fingers.

Shane and Mickey led the charge through the wide doorway. Shane fired as quickly as he could, pushing deeper into the room filled with hostiles to create space for the rest of his team to get inside. The room was illuminated with the flashing light of the muzzles. Shane dropped down behind one of the peacekeepers he'd killed, using his body as a shield. Soon, Shane's team had control of the area. He saw Abdulov cut out the side door. Shane sprung up from his position and gave chase.

Abdulov sprinted down the hallway until he came to another stairway which had been taken out by the tank round. He quickly turned and aimed his AK-47 at Shane.

However, Shane already had him in his sights. He pulled the trigger hitting him in the forehead. The commander dropped backward, tumbling down the stairs, then falling on his back to the floor below.

CHAPTER 21

"If you do not control the enemy, the enemy will control you."

Miyamoto Musashi, A Book of Five Rings

A voice came over the radio. "Shane! This is Jimmy. The peacekeepers at the hotel were taking potshots at us, but now they're trying to get out and make a run for it. It's more than we can keep contained. I need some help over here!"

Shane turned to see Mickey behind him. "Did you get that?"

"Yep. I'll get the tank headed in that direction if you want to check on your buddy."

"Okay." Shane pressed the talk key. "Help is on the way." He sprinted back to the scene of the last skirmish. Two bikers and one man from Sylva had been killed. Shane found Julianna helping one of Mickey's men toward the stairs. He'd been shot in the knee and was in a great amount of pain. Shane put his arm under the man's other shoulder. "Come on. We have to get you down the stairs so a medic can look at you." They hurried him to the broken stairwell.

Shane and Julianna handed the man down to other people waiting to receive him below. Next, Shane let himself down, dangling from the rail. He let go and broke his fall by letting his knees buckle beneath himself. He stood back up and held out his hands to Julianna. "Let go. I'll catch you."

She released her grip of the rail and fell into Shane's arms. The two of them tumbled to the ground. Before letting her go, he asked, "Are you okay?"

She turned, looked into his eyes and nodded. "Yeah, I'm good."

Even though they had no less than twenty on-lookers, Shane could have been content to stay in that position forever. However, he had a mission to complete. Shane pushed her into an upright position and the two of them got off the floor and headed to the place where they'd left Bobby.

A medic had conscripted another fighter to assist him in caring for Bobby's wound.

"Is he going to be okay?" Julianna asked.

"He'll be alright," the medic replied. "As soon as we can confirm that we have control of Sylva, we'll move him to the hospital so we can get him stitched up."

Shane gave Bobby's shoulder a squeeze. "I think

it's safe to say the town is ours, but we've got a couple more rats to kill. We'll come to the hospital when we're done."

"Do what you have to do," said Bobby.

Once outside, Shane found Wrench behind the wheel of one of the UN armored vehicles. The old biker leaned out the window. "Need a ride?"

"Yeah." Shane helped Julianna inside the armored personnel carrier. Butterbean was inside along with five other Hill Runners.

Shane pointed forward. "Take us through town instead of back on the expressway."

Wrench drove out of the parking lot and toward the hotel. "These trucks aren't half bad, but I think I'd have chosen another color besides white."

"You're set up to paint in your shop, aren't you?" asked Julianna.

"Motorcycles," replied the old biker. "It'd be a bigger job than what I'm used to, but I suppose I could swing it."

Shane called over the radio. "Jimmy, the tank and several more shooters are coming your way. I need to make a pit stop. Think you can handle things until we get there?"

"I see the tank now. We'll be okay."

"We'll see you shortly," said Shane.

"Where to?" asked Wrench.

"The big white house on Haywood Road. The one right before we get to the hotel. That's Wallace Hayes' house. I'm guessing we'll find Lurch there also. Maybe Rita Carmichael, too."

Wrench said, "You should've had the tank level it on the way over. One shell would probably turn the entire house into a pile of rubble."

"Yeah, I thought about that," said Shane. "But he has a little girl. I'm pretty sure she's at his property up on the mountain, but I want to be sure."

Wrench slowed down when they reached the old white house. "Six UN troops standing out front. They must be guarding something."

Julianna pointed at the ceiling. "We've got a .50 cal up top. That would make them scatter."

"Any of you know how to run it?" Shane looked at the bikers in the back of the vehicle.

All shook their heads.

"I've got experience with them," said Julianna.

Shane recalled their narrow escape from Harvey Hammer's prison. "Okay. Wrench, stay with Julianna. Help her reload if necessary. Everyone else, follow me as soon as the action starts."

Julianna climbed up into the turret and began firing.

Shane threw the door open. "That's our cue." He led the charge up the stairs to the porch. He ran to the side and gunned down the only two troops who'd escaped Julianna's fusillade. Next, he shot the lock of the door and kicked it open. He led his team from room to room, but no one was on the first floor.

"Upstairs." Shane was the first one up the steps. He checked the first two rooms but found nobody. He kicked in the last door.

Wallace Hayes stood just inside with his pistol pointed at Shane's head. "Put down your gun. Call off your troops."

Shane lined up the red dot with Hayes' forehead.

"Why would I do that?"

A gunshot rang from outside. Hayes grinned. "Because I don't see that pretty little redhead with you. And I'm betting if you look out that window, you'll see that Mr. Hicks has a gun to her head. Put down your rifle, or you'll both die."

"Check it out," Shane called to Butterbean.

"Yep. He's shot Wrench, and he's got Julianna," said the robust former deputy.

Shane walked closer and closer to Hayes. "No way. We're not giving up."

Hayes grin turned downward. "I'm not bluffing." Still pointing the pistol at Shane, his hands shook.

"I don't care. If you pull that trigger, I'll pull this one. I don't want to lose Julianna, but we're not going to live as slaves. Not anymore." Once he was close enough, Shane slung the butt of his rifle and struck Hayes in the cheek. Hayes fell to the ground and Shane jumped on top of him, wrestling the pistol from his hand. "Get up!"

Shane grabbed Wallace Hayes by his shirt collar. He drew his own pistol and placed it at the nape of Hayes' neck. "Walk." Shane escorted him down the stairs to the street. Butterbean and the rest of the Hill Runners followed him.

"Looks like we've got a stalemate." Lurch held Julianna by the hair, his pistol pointed at her back.

"I'm open to a trade," said Shane.

"Not a chance," said Lurch. "The second we turn our backs, your men will gun us down. Here's how this is going to work. You let Wallace go. We'll get out of town and leave Julianna somewhere safe. We'll leave a radio a mile up the road. She can walk to the radio and call you to come pick her up."

"Don't do it, Shane. Kill them. Kill them both!" Julianna yelled.

"Shut up!" Lurch jerked her backward by the hair.

Shane saw that the pistol pointed at her back had moved off target when Lurch pulled her. He knew this was his only opportunity. He fired at Lurch. The bullet hit Lurch between the right eye and the nose, killing him instantaneously—almost.

Lurch's gun discharged. The projectile ripped through Julianna, spraying blood in its wake. Both she and Lurch fell to the ground.

"Julianna!" Shane screamed in horror. He pushed Hayes out of his way, dropped to his knees beside her, and watched her blood pour out on to the pavement. He gently put his hand under her head. "Julianna, please, don't leave me."

Her chest was soaked in blood, yet her eyes flicked open for a moment. She gasped in anguish. "It hurts."

Just then, Wallace Hayes scrambled toward Lurch's pistol which had skidded to the middle of the street. Shane wanted so badly to ignore the threat. He couldn't rip his eyes away from Julianna in this precarious moment, not even for a second.

Butterbean shot Hayes in the back while one of the Hill Runners kicked away the pistol and put his boot on Hayes' wrist.

Shane took out his knife and cut away the left side of her shirt. He quickly located the wound and pressed a packet of Quickclot onto the exit wound. "It's high. I don't think it could have hit any vital organs. But we need to control this bleeding." Shane motioned to Butterbean. "I need you to keep pressure on this sponge while I lift her up and get another one on the entry wound."

"Sure." Butterbean complied with Shane's request.

Julianna gritted her teeth when Shane lifted her torso to look at her back. Shane ripped open a second packet of Quickclot. "The pain means you're still alive." He pressed the hemostatic agent against the entry wound when he located it. Then, he wrapped a compression bandage around her chest to hold both Quickclot sponges in place.

"Okay, we need to get her in the back of the armored vehicle," Shane said to Butterbean. "You grab her feet, and I'll grab her shoulders."

Shane tried to lift with more pressure on the side where she'd not been shot but had to grab beneath the bullet wound as well.

"Ahhh!" she cried. "No, Shane! I think I can walk. I can't take the pain of you putting your arm under the left shoulder."

"Okay, let's try walking." He nodded to Butterbean.

Julianna bit her lip as she struggled to stand on her own and walk to the truck. However, she made it inside.

"This guy is still alive out here," said one of the bikers. "What are we going to do with him?"

Shane couldn't concentrate on Wallace Hayes at the moment. "Bring him with us. We'll figure out what to do with him after we get Julianna to the hospital."

A big burly biker carried Hayes into the vehicle and another of the Hill Runners drove the armored personnel carrier to the hospital.

"I'm so sorry," said Shane.

Julianna closed her eyes and shook her head. "You did the right thing. If you hadn't shot Lurch, this thing would never be over." She opened her eyes and put her hand on his cheek. "No matter what happens to me, you did the right thing."

His mouth contorted in sorrow, still worrying that her life was in the balance.

She forced a smile through her suffering. Her voice grew faint. "Tell me you know that. Tell me you did the right thing."

He painted on a happy face. His lips quivered, his words cracked. "I did the right thing."

When they arrived at the hospital Julianna was drifting in and out of consciousness. Shane rushed inside and found a wheelchair with which to move her. Butterbean assisted him in getting her into the chair, then Shane rushed in. He quickly looked for someone he might recognize. "Janie!"

Johnny Teague's daughter turned around to see him. "We've got another gunshot victim!" She rushed to Julianna's side. "I'll take her from here, Shane. We're completely inundated with patients. More casualties than doctors, but I'll make sure Julianna gets treated first."

"Thank you!" he said. "Thank you for helping out. Lisa Bivens knows Julianna. If she's here, I'm sure she'll help, at least to get her stabilized. I need to get back to the fight. It's not over yet."

Julianna was completely unconscious. Shane

swallowed hard and kissed her on the lips. He prayed silently to God that it would not be the last time he ever got the chance to do so.

"Go. Do what you have to do. I'll take care of Julianna." Janie smiled and wheeled Julianna toward the overwhelmed trauma unit.

Shane and Butterbean rushed back to the vehicle. He threw open the door and glared at Wallace Hayes. "This is all your fault."

Hayes was breathing heavily and obviously in great pain from his injury. "Shane, I had nothing to do with the UN taking over Sylva."

"No, but you sure didn't make a fuss about being reinstated."

"What was I supposed to do? They insisted."

"Your henchman shot Julianna. She's fighting for her life right now." Shane drew his pistol. "Because of you."

"Our backs were against the wall." Hayes held up his hand. "We were trying to bargain to stay alive! You'd have done the same thing in my position." Hayes seemed weak. "Please, take me inside. I need to see a doctor."

"You chose the wrong side. I'm not going to burden the hospital staff with your sorry bag of bones. In fact, I'm debating whether or not to put you down right here and now."

"No, Shane, please."

Shane put the barrel of his gun under Hayes' chin. "Then convince me that you have something of value. What will you give me in return for your pathetic life?"

"Anything. What do you want?"

"Where is Rita Carmichael?"

"I don't know."

Shane shoved the gun tighter against his throat. "Then you're no good to me."

"Wait!" Hayes pleaded. "She took over a cabin. A big one, up on Watershed Way. But I doubt she's still there. She had a security staff of eight peacekeepers. I'm sure they moved her when the shooting started. They recommend that I move. I had nowhere to go except my compound. Evelyn and Gina are there. I knew if I left, you'd find me. I didn't want to lead you there, so I stayed at the house."

"Okay. Let's go see. If you're telling me the truth, I won't kill you." Shane got in the vehicle. "Tell the driver how to get there."

"And you'll take me back to the hospital?"

"After all our injured have been treated, I'll take you back to the hospital." Shane closed the door and the driver followed Hayes' directions.

Upon their arrival, Shane led Butterbean and the bikers out with rifles ready to fire. "Be alert. We could be up against twenty peacekeepers or the place could be abandoned." Both garage doors were open and neither of them had vehicles inside. Shane led the team in through the garage, then into the kitchen area which was unlocked.

"I don't see anything," said Butterbean.

"Let's not count our chickens just yet." Shane led the men through the rest of the house, clearing each room before proceeding further. "Looks like they left in a hurry." He lowered his rifle after searching the last room. "They left clothing, shoes, stuff everywhere."

"This is a big fine house," the big burly biker said. "If ain't nobody using it, a few of us might feel right at home here."

Shane looked around. "I suppose that would be okay. If the owners ever show up, you'll have to vacate right away."

"I wouldn't think of stayin' if the owners showed up," he said.

Shane pressed the talk key. "Jimmy, how are things looking at the hotel?"

"We got a couple of superficial wounds. Nobody killed. At least not from our side. Things didn't turn out so well for the UN troops. We've got a tattooed broad over here. Evidently, she was sleeping around behind Greg's back with one of the peacekeepers."

"Tessa?" Shane asked. "Is she still alive?"

"Ain't none of 'em alive," Jimmy replied. "I guess it's all for the best. Poor Greg would have lost his head if he'd have found out."

Shane grimaced and pressed the talk key once more. "That's not funny. You didn't see it for yourself. It was the nastiest thing I've seen in all my life."

"One of the boys told me about it. I couldn't resist," laughed Jimmy. "Anyhow, did you find Hayes?"

"Yeah. He's got a bullet in the torso. I killed Hicks. Julianna was shot during the operation."

"I'm so sorry. Is she going to be okay?"

"I don't know. If you don't need me, I'm going to head on back to the hospital."

"I don't need you over here. We're going

through their stuff. Seeing what we can salvage of value before we start the big bonfire. Where are you now?"

"Up on Watershed Way; the place where Rita Carmichael was staying. She's flown the coop."

"Okay then. I'll see you when I see you. We beat 'em, Shane."

Shane allowed himself to relish the victory for the smallest moment. "Yeah—for now."

CHAPTER 22

Blessed is the man that walketh not in the counsel of the ungodly, nor standeth in the way of sinners, nor sitteth in the seat of the scornful. But his delight is in the law of the Lord; and in his law doth he meditate day and night. And he shall be like a tree planted by the rivers of water, that bringeth forth his fruit in his season; his leaf also shall not wither; and whatsoever he doeth shall prosper. The ungodly are not so: but are like the chaff which the wind driveth away. Therefore the ungodly shall not stand in the judgment, nor sinners in the congregation of the righteous. For the Lord knoweth the way of the righteous: but the way of the ungodly shall perish.

Psalm 1

Two days later, Shane sat in the middle of the porch swing at the little house. Julianna sat on his right with a sling around her left arm. Cole sat on his left. Shane let his hand rest gently on Julianna's neck. His other arm was around his son, pulling him close.

"Shane was a mess over you at the hospital, Julianna. I've never seen him so distraught." Bobby sat on the stairs with his leg heavily bandaged and his arm around Angela.

Shane looked at Julianna's dressings. "The bullet cracked her collar bone. Nicked the blood vessel coming off her subclavian artery. That's why she was in so much pain and lost so much blood."

"It looked worse than it actually was." Julianna looked over at Cole as if to comfort him.

Shane thought about how close he'd come to losing her. "If it had been an inch lower and hit the subclavian, it would have been a much worse situation."

"You're stuck with me until God gets ready to call me home." She smiled and put her hand on Shane's knee.

"Elizabeth Hayes left early this morning," said Angela.

"Where to?" asked Bobby.

Angela leaned against Bobby. "She's moving out to the big lodge on Breakstone Ridge with her sister-in- law, Gina, and her niece, Evelyn. With their husbands both gone, Elizabeth and Gina can provide mutual support for one another. She took Sorghum with her."

Shane thought about Wallace Hayes. He'd taken the man back to the hospital as he'd promised, but Hayes had already bled out when they arrived. "I told Elizabeth to let me know if they needed anything. Neither Gina nor Evelyn would accept anything coming directly from me, but if it comes from Elizabeth, they'll never know."

"That's good of you," Julianna said.

"I hear Butterbean put his name in the hat for sheriff," Bobby laughed.

"Yeah," said Shane with a chuckle. "Jimmy is trying to get him to be content with being appointed head jailer."

"Is that even a title?" Julianna asked.

"It is now," Shane replied. "Jimmy made it up. Butterbean has gone above and beyond the call of duty and deserves some type of recognition. However, the job of sheriff might be a little more challenging than what Butterbean is ready for."

Angela asked, "Kari and Scott aren't planning to stay out in Murphy are they?"

"No," Shane answered. "They're going back to their old homestead for now. I told Kari that they'd always have a place here. She promised that they would come back if Jackson County ever comes under threat of violence again. But I can understand her wanting to get back to their own land."

Moments later, Angela looked up at her brother. "You're not mad at me, are you?"

"About what?"

She glanced at Bobby, then back to Shane.

Shane eyed her and Bobby. "About my sister and best friend getting married? Why would I be angry about that? A little surprised maybe, but not mad. I'm happy for you."

"Good." She leaned closer to Bobby then asked, "So, when are you two getting hitched?"

Shane braced himself in expectation of Julianna's stern response. He couldn't believe his sister would bring up such a sore subject.

"Never!" Julianna exclaimed in a snap.

"Ouch!" Bobby winced.

It was the reply he'd anticipated, but it still cut Shane to the core. While he allowed himself very little time for daydreaming about what a life with Julianna would be like, neither did he dwell on the frigid reality that they could never be together.

She grinned playfully at Shane. "Yeah, it seems like he's never going to ask—and call me old fashioned, but I'm certainly not going to be the one to do it."

Shane mulled the sentence over and over in his mind. *Is she joking? Did I hear her correctly? What am I missing?* Finally, he looked up. With caution, he examined her face which still bore the same mischievous smile.

However, the corners of her mouth continued to migrate in an upward direction. Her cheeks took on a radiant glow. Still babying her injury, she leaned over, puckered her lips and kissed Shane on the mouth.

He felt cold, then hot, then dizzy, as if he might pass out. An ocean of emotion raged inside of him.

Once he was sure that he wasn't going to fall out of the swing, he gripped the back of her neck tenderly. He kissed her once more, long, and passionately.

Finally, she pulled back, ran her thumb along her bottom lip, and grinned.

Shane stared into her eyes, then glanced at his son.

Cole sat beside him, his eyes as wide as coffee cans, his mouth hanging open like a barn door caught by the wind. "Are…are… are you going to marry Mama?" the young boy demanded.

Shane turned back to her. "Julianna, will you marry me?"

Her smile grew. Her cheeks went from pink to red. "Yes." She nodded adamantly. "Yes, Shane. I'll marry you."

DON'T PANIC!

Inevitably, books like this will wake folks up to the need to be prepared, or cause those of us who are already prepared to take inventory of our preparations. New preppers can find the task of getting prepared for an economic collapse, EMP, or societal breakdown to be a source of great anxiety. It shouldn't be. By following an organized plan and setting a goal of getting a little more prepared each day, you can do it.

I always try to include a few prepper tips in my novels, but they're fiction and not a comprehensive plan to get prepared. Now that you're motivated to start prepping, the last thing I want to do is leave you frustrated, not knowing what to do next. So I'd like to offer you a free PDF copy of *The Seven Step Survival Plan.*

For the new prepper, *The Seven Step Survival Plan* provides a blueprint that prioritizes the different aspects of preparedness and breaks them down into achievable goals. For seasoned preppers who often get overweight in one particular area of preparedness, *The Seven Step Survival Plan* provides basic guidelines to help keep their plan in balance, and ensures they're not missing any critical segments of a well-adjusted survival strategy.

To get your **FREE** copy of ***The Seven Step Survival Plan***, go to **PrepperRecon.com** and click the FREE PDF banner, just below the menu bar, at the top of the home page.

Thank you for reading
Black Swan, Book Three: Gehenna

If you liked the book, please take a moment to leave a review. It helps more than you can imagine.

I love hearing from readers! So whether it's to say you enjoyed the book, to point out a typo that we missed, or asked to be notified when new books are released, drop me a line.

prepperrecon@gmail.com

Stay tuned to **PrepperRecon.com** for the latest news about my upcoming books.

Keep watch for my upcoming series,

The Beginning of Sorrows, A Saga of the End Times

Can't get enough post-apocalyptic chaos? Check out my other heart-stopping tales about the end of the world as we know it.

The Days of Noah

In an off-site CIA facility outside of Langley, rookie analyst Everett Carroll discovers he's not being told the whole truth. He's instructed to disregard troubling information uncovered by his research. Everett ignores his directive and keeps digging. What he finds goes against everything he's been taught to believe. Unfortunately, his curiosity doesn't escape the attention of his superiors, and it may cost him his life.

Meanwhile, Tennessee public school teacher, Noah Parker, like many in the United States, has been asleep at the wheel. During his complacency, the founding precepts of America have been systematically destroyed by a conspiracy that dates back hundreds of years.

Cassandra Parker, Noah's wife, has diligently followed end-times prophecy and the shifting tide against freedom in America. Noah has tried to avoid the subject, but when charges are filed against him for deviating from the approved curriculum in his school, he quickly understands the seriousness of the situation. The signs can no longer be ignored, and Noah is forced to prepare for the cataclysmic period of financial and political upheaval ahead.

Watch through the eyes of Noah Parker and Everett Carroll as the world descends into chaos, a global empire takes shape, ancient writings are fulfilled, and the last days fall upon the once-great United States of America.

Seven Cows, Ugly and Gaunt

In **Book One: Behold Darkness and Sorrow**, Daniel Walker begins having prophetic dreams about the judgment coming upon America for rejecting God. Through one of his dreams, Daniel learns of an imminent threat of an EMP attack which will wipe out America's electric grid and most all computerized devices, sending the country into a technological dark age.

Living in a nation where all life-sustaining systems of support are completely dependent on electricity and computers, the odds of survival are dismal. Municipal water services, retail food distribution, police, fire, EMS and all emergency services will come to a screeching halt.

If they want to live, Daniel and his friends must focus on faith, wits, and preparation to be ready . . . before the lights go out.

Cyber Armageddon

Cyber Security Analyst Kate McCarthy knows something ominous is about to happen in the US banking system. She has a place to go if things get hectic, but it's far from the perfect retreat.

When a new breed of computer virus takes down America's financial network, chaos and violence erupt. Access to cash disappears and credit cards become worthless. Desperate consumers are left with no means to purchase food, fuel, and basic necessities. Society melts down instantly and the threat of starvation brings out the absolute worst humanity has to offer.

In the midst of the mayhem, Kate will face a post-apocalyptic nightmare that she never could have imagined. Her only reward for survival is to live another day in the gruesome new reality which has eradicated the world she once knew.

Ava's Crucible

The deck is stacked against twenty-nine-year-old Ava. She's a fighter, but she's got trust issues and doesn't always make the best decisions. Her personal complications aren't without merit, but America is on the verge of a second civil war, and Ava must pull it together if she wants to survive.

The tentacles of the deep state have infiltrated every facet of American culture. The public education system, entertainment industry, and mainstream media have all been hijacked by a shadow government intent on fomenting a communist revolution in the United States. The antagonistic message of this agenda has poisoned the minds of America's youth who are convinced that capitalism and conservatism are responsible for all the ills of the world. Violent protest, widespread destruction, and politicians who insist on letting the disassociated vent their rage will bring America to her knees, threatening to decapitate the laws, principles, and values on which the country was founded. The revolution has been well-planned, but the socialists may have underestimated America's true patriots who refuse to give up without a fight.

ABOUT THE AUTHOR

Mark Goodwin holds a degree in accounting and monitors macroeconomic conditions to stay up-to-date with the ongoing global meltdown.

He is an avid student of the Holy Bible and spends several hours every week devoted to the study of Scripture and the prophecies contained therein.

The troubling trends in the moral, social, political, and financial landscapes have prompted Mark to conduct extensive research within the arena of preparedness.

He weaves his knowledge of biblical prophecy, economics, politics, prepping, and survival into an action-packed tapestry of post-apocalyptic fiction. Having been a sinner saved by grace himself, the story of redemption is a prominent theme in all of Mark's writings.

"He brought me up also out of an horrible pit, out of the miry clay, and set my feet upon a rock, and established my goings." Psalm 40:2